MADE TO LOVE HER

MAGGIE & VINCE, #2

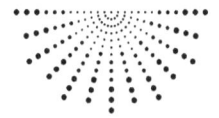

Z.L. ARKADIE

Z.L. ARKADIE BOOKS

ISBN: 978-1-942857-86-0

❀ Created with Vellum

ACKNOWLEDGMENTS

Thanks to the following:

Edited by Red Adept Editing

Cover Design by Cover Couture

CHAPTER ONE

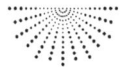

MAGGIE CONROY

I sigh heavily. This is my first answer to Maddie's or Allie's question—I still can't tell Vince's sisters apart. There are three of them—Lexie, Maddie and Allie. Each has bleached blond hair, a tiny mousy face and speaks in high-pitched voice that gives me a headache. At least now I only have to contend with two of them. We're back at the bakery. We were here yesterday for six hours. One of Vince's sisters—Lexie, I think—stomped out in a huff because I didn't want a wedding cake with red roses on top. I didn't care if they tasted like cherry meringue. I don't know much about weddings, but I do know enough to realize that red roses do not go on top of wedding cakes, at least not the non-tacky ones. I feel as if they have been trying to sabotage me from the beginning. Today is Tuesday. We started the whole wedding planning process from hell together Monday of last week. We've been aided by a mysterious wedding planner named Lily, whom I've yet to meet. The only reason I believe she exists is that lying to me about her would be an elaborate scheme. Vince's clan can't really hate me that much. Could they?

The wedding cake specialist rubs her brow as if to ward off the same headache that I have. "So, Maggie, are you ready to make your final decision on the top tier?"

This is our second day of taste-testing cakes and selecting fillings. I'm starting to think that we've eaten enough cake to compose one gigantic wedding cake.

I open my mouth to speak but Vince's sister throws her hand up in front of my face in a pretty rude manner. "Lily wholeheartedly suggests the chocolate layer on top," Maddie says. I'm pretty sure she's Maddie, the one who always wears the white pearl earrings.

"But I don't like chocolate cake, and neither does Vince. What's wrong with all-white cake with buttercream frosting?" I say.

She blows sharply through her nose. "Vince does like chocolate cake."

"No. He does not." I check my watch. I can't believe that I'm participating in an argument over cake.

Speaking of Vince, I'm pissed to the umpteenth power at him. He was supposed to arrive yesterday at eight o'clock. I've been trying to call him for the last eighteen hours. At first, the phone rang three times then went to voicemail. Now my calls go straight to voicemail. I might have thought he was cheating on me if I didn't know for certain he wouldn't do that. Before flying out to Denver, we spent three beautiful weeks together in Hawaii. Vince and I had the time of our lives. Instead of fighting LA traffic and rushing to staff meetings, we did sunset yoga every morning and paddle-boarded afterward. Each day, Vince flew us to a new island in his helicopter. That was one of many new things I learned about him on our trip—he has his pilot's license. We explored the volcanoes, tropical forests, and beaches like there was no tomorrow. At night, I would throw on a tank dress and flip-flops and Vince would wear Bermuda shorts and a T-shirt. Then we would drink mai tais at a tiki bar by the beach. For the most part, we kept busy surfing, dancing, mountain climbing, hiking, and swimming —doing anything but making love. It's been so very difficult to keep the pact to not make love until after the wedding. I had to keep reminding myself that celibacy was my very bad idea. I almost reneged on it more times than I can remember.

"Excuse me, but can I have your complete and undivided attention just for this one moment please," the sister says.

Thank goodness I'm not one for turning red, but I've had it up to my eyeballs with their rudeness. I think back to the promise I made to Vince: I would be cordial no matter how far they pushed me. At least he hadn't tried to convince me that his sisters would be a joy to be around. They hate the fact that I'm marrying their brother. When he called to invite them to the small ceremony I was planning in Southampton, New York, his mother, Anne, nearly choked on her gasps. By the end of their conversation, she had laid such a guilt trip on Vince that he convinced me to have the ceremony in Denver and to let his sisters and mother help plan it. That was on a Friday. On Sunday, we flew to Denver. They had me scheduled for dress fittings on Monday morning. Every single dress the saleswoman showed me was horrendous. On Tuesday, she showed me another load of frumpy dresses, and Wednesday was the same. Thursday, I called one of my best friends, Hannah, who's a professional fashion stylist. She gave me the name and address of a friend of hers who owns a boutique downtown.

I left early that morning to meet Kara Zane of Zane Dress Studio, which is located downtown. I tried on two gorgeous dresses before I discovered the perfect one. Of course, the sisters were angry that I found a dress without them, and they ratcheted up their passive-aggressive campaign.

On top of that, Vince flew back to New York later that day. A photo surfaced of Reno Nelson, the lead actor of the *Firescape* sci-fi/action thriller series, kneeling over a dead rhinoceros, with a rifle tucked under his arm. As a result, every single advertiser of the television show pulled out. I was still fighting the urge to fly to New York to figure out the fastest way to save the show. But the incident was too close to home. It felt like a Mo&Ma matter, and I'm just not ready to go back to shoveling the shit high-profile people find themselves buried under.

However, at the moment something clicks inside me. I'm looking into the sister's eyes, and I see her disdain looking back at me. How many times have I handled difficult clients like Maddie or Allie? The trick is to not smile—not yet.

I calmly stuff my phone back into my purse and make sure I'm not looking at her as if I think she's a crazy person. I place a hand on my chest. "Listen, I like chocolate cake," I lie. "Vince, however, doesn't have many requests regarding the planning of this wedding, but not having chocolate wedding cake is one of them. So let's just do no chocolate cake for him. He deserves it, don't you think?"

The sisters look at each other. They have a way of communicating with their facial expressions, and I'm starting to decipher them. I guess it's my survival instincts. Their raised eyebrows prove what I thought. They've been screwing with my head, which is easy for them to do now that Vince isn't here to side with me.

One of the sisters grunts as if she's just been defeated. "Okay."

The other scratches the back of her head. "Maddie, let's just get all white with lemon cream at the top, white chocolate mousse filling in tier two, strawberry glaze for tier three, and blueberry compote at the bottom and be done with it."

Maddie glances at me then puts her hand over

the receiver. "But that's not what Lily wants," she whispers.

I ready my lips to say, "Fuck Lily!" This is my wedding not hers.

But Allie whispers, "Screw Lily" instead. "At least on this. Vince likes all those fillings." Allie crosses her arms defiantly. "I'm going with what Vince likes on this one. Period."

I raise my eyebrows, intrigued. I think I may have discovered an ally, and her name is Allie.

Maddie tells the wedding planner that we have the whole cake situation under control then hangs up the phone. We confirm the cake filling along with the white cake for the top three tiers and chocolate cake at the bottom. I would still rather have all-white cake and buttercream frosting, but I figure we all have to compromise—even if I've been doing most of the settling.

THE CAR RIDE BACK TO THE HOUSE IS AWKWARD. AT least this time, it's quieter than usual. Maddie is clearly peeved at Allie for giving in so easily. I may have won the cake war, but I plan on trying to talk Vince into eloping.

As we're arriving back at Anne's house, we pass

a cab on its way out. My back hugs the seat as I sigh in relief. Vince must've made it back. Oh boy, does he have a lot of explaining to do. The car stops, and we all jump out as fast as we can and rush inside. Apparently, I'm not the only one excited to see Vince. Before the first one of us makes it to the steps, a uniquely pretty woman with short hair and a heart-shaped face steps out of the front door, waving.

Disappointed, I stop in my tracks.

The woman holds her arms out to take a hug from Allie, while studying me curiously. "I made it!"

"Carter, you made it," Allie says.

They hug.

"Is Vince here?" I ask before realizing what I said.

Suddenly, like an angel in the sky, Vince walks out of the house and stands beside her.

He and I grin at each other. I swear it's as if this is the first time we ever locked eyes.

I walk past the woman named Carter and bury my face in Vince's chest. The way he smells… The warmth rising from his body… Gosh, I'm so happy to see him that I want to cry.

"I've been trying to call you," I say.

He plants a strong kiss on my forehead and then

my lips. "Sorry, babe, I lost my phone. New York was crazy. A town car almost hit me, and my chartered flight was grounded due to mechanical issues, so I had to take a commercial flight." He scratches the back of his neck. "The best part was I ran into this one at the airport." He points his thumb at Carter, and she smiles. "This is my cousin, Carter."

I smile, and she smiles back. It's a huge relief to finally get a genuinely warm expression from someone in Vince's family.

"Well, I'm going in the house. But, Carter, we have to talk, so hurry up and get your tush inside," Allie says. She rubs Vince on the arm. "Glad you're back."

He kisses her on the cheek. "Glad to be back."

Allie smiles tightly at me before trotting up the steps and into the house. That was unusual. She normally pretends as if I'm not here.

"Nice to meet you, Maggie. Vince told me a lot about you," Carter says.

I shake her hand. "I hope he said great things."

"He basically said you were smart, ambitious, and beautiful—a triple threat."

"Wow, that *is* great."

She chuckles. "I would say so."

Vince rolls his eyes playfully. "Oh, come on, I

said more than that, Carly."

"Hey," Carter grouses.

Vince laughs and looks at me. "I used to call her Carly for fun."

"Yeah, because Robert Tango could never remember my name, and Vince never corrected him."

"Hey, I thought Carly had a certain ring to it."

She rolls her eyes hard. "No, it doesn't."

We look at each other after the laughter simmers and good vibrations surround us.

"Anyway, I'm here to help you in whatever way I can," Carter says to me. The look in her eyes tells me that she senses what I've been going through with Maddie, Allie, and Lexie.

"Thank you," I say in a sincere tone.

"You're welcome."

WE GO INSIDE. DINNER IS IN TWO HOURS, AND before Vince and I head upstairs to freshen up, Lexie, who hasn't said a word to me since the beginning of Wedding Dress-gate last week, tells us that Lily will be joining us for dinner. Finally, I'll get to meet the mysterious Lily.

Vince and I make it to his old bedroom, and he

shuts the door behind us. We kick off our shoes, wrap our arms around each other, and fall onto the bed, kissing. Our mouths go at it feverishly. It's just so good to taste him, feel him, and hear him groan with pleasure again. My nether regions throb for us to take this session to the next step. Vince slides his finger against my clit through my silky panties.

"Baby," he sighs.

"I know… screw it," I whisper thickly.

Vince's tongue dives deeper into my mouth. My head is spinning. He separates my knees and tugs at the clasps and zipper of his pants. I'm wet with anticipation. Then there's a loud gasp.

Vince and I turn our fiery gazes toward the door.

His mom is standing at the threshold, a stack of fluffy royal-blue bath towels at her feet. "Um…" Anne puts a hand over her eyes. "These are for you." She squats with her eyes closed and feels for the towels.

Vince springs off the bed while zipping his pants. "I'll get them, Mom."

I grab a pillow, wanting to bury my face in it, but the show is far too awkward to miss.

Anne stands up and steps back, banging into the wall. "Okay."

Vince bends down to pick up the towels. "Mom, you should've knocked."

"You're right, son. But next time, could you please lock the door?"

"Yes. I will." He stands and looks at her for a moment. "Mom?"

Her eyes are still closed. "Yes."

"You can open your eyes."

She slowly opens her eyes and glances at me. I pull my legs up to my chest and hug them tightly. I feel as if I should apologize for leading her son down to the den of sex, lust, and all the dirty things she never pictured him doing.

Her gaze flicks to Vince. The way she's looking at him… It's as if she's seeing him in a different light. "Sorry, honey. I'll see you both at dinner."

Anne backs out of the room, closing the door behind her.

Vince stands still. He's still discombobulated by what happened. "Okay, tomorrow, we're in a suite at the Ritz-Carlton." He flexes his eyebrows at me. "Especially if we're back on." He dives onto the bed. "Now where was I?"

I squirm out of Vince's grasp. "Wait a minute." His erection is rigid and ready to dive into my wetness.

"Come on, Maggie," he groans.

I roll off the bed to stand. "Maybe she stopped us for reason. We've gotten this far."

"Baby, let's stop this nonsense." He scoots off the bed and throws his hands up. "This is me, thoroughly sexually frustrated."

"Well, I am too, but I've been thinking."

He rolls his eyes. "What now?"

"Let's just elope. That way, no one gets slighted. We don't have the wedding in Southampton, where I want it, or here, where your sisters and mother have been giving me hell."

Vince tilts his head and studies me sympathetically for a moment. "Has it gotten worse since I've been gone?"

"All the way until the end of today."

"What happened at the end of today?"

I tell him about my minor cake victory—how in a split second, I decided to treat his sisters like my difficult and spoiled former celebrity clients, and it worked.

"Of course I can continue to handle your family like they're a special case, but I've really had it up to here with them and the mysterious Lily."

"Lily? Who's that?"

"Remember, the mysterious wedding planner."

"Oh." He nods. "Right."

I scrunch up my nose. "I think they're all in it together."

Vince sighs and pulls me in closer. "Carter said there might be some supplanting going on."

Just hearing my suspicions confirmed makes me regret ever being gracious enough to give them a chance to plan *my* wedding, which is supposed to be *my* big day, not theirs. "Jeez. What's wrong with them?"

"That's the million-dollar question, sweetie." He beams as if he's been injected with a sudden dose of optimism. "The good news is that Carter promised to try to contain them for you."

I groan and flail my body, pouting like a five year old. "Vince, why don't we just get the hell out of here?"

He takes a long sigh. "Listen, if we don't get through this, I'll never hear the end of it, and you'll always be the enemy."

I want to dig in and hold my position, but I fight the urge to do it. People are my specialty, and Vince is one hundred percent correct. Part of me doesn't give a damn if they hate me forever. The other part would prefer to live in harmony with Vince's family.

"Well, at least can we stay at the Ritz-Carlton?

After what just happened with Anne, I think that's enough to justify our escape."

Vince sits on the side of the bed and starts taking off his socks. "I think that's reasonable. Plus, this house is going to be packed out starting tomorrow when the wedding party comes to town."

The thought makes me sigh wearily. The house is already full, as it is. The large property has two casitas in the back, and one has its own in-ground hot tub. One of Vince's sisters and her husband are staying in that one. Another sister is staying in the second casita. Allie, who still lives at home until she marries her fiancé in September, is staying in a room on the third level, way at the end of the hallway. I think they planned to put distance between themselves and me while not allowing Vince and me to indulge in our own privacy. But they ended up helping us out. Since we weren't so isolated, being that Anne's room is right above ours, we didn't act on our impulses. This whole "let's wait until after we're married" pact has almost been ripped to shreds more times than I can count. However, spending late nights in bed, sharing how difficult things were after each of our parents divorced and me growing up as an only child and him growing up with three overbearing sisters made us closer. We even vegged out on all the TV shows and movies we'd missed while working too hard over the past three years. But I've spent a week of tiptoeing around Vince's mother's house, making sure I make breakfast by eight in the morning and round up his sisters to go downtown to follow through with wedding plans by ten. Then there's dinner, when everyone but Anne pretends I'm invisible. I often wonder if she's aware of what her daughters are up to. She hasn't accompanied us to any of the dress fittings, the cake tasting, or the "luxury" ranch where the wedding ceremony and reception are to be held. However, whenever we sit at the table and the sisters relay what we've done for the day, Anne seems very excited and pleased with their choices. I mean, a barn? I don't really want to get married in a barn. I haven't fought them all as hard as I could because I'm not especially interested in going to battle with Vince's mother. And deep down, I've been hoping that Vince will agree to elope.

I grunt thoughtfully.

"What is it?" Vince says.

I watch him with one eye narrowed. No need to divulge my great epiphany. I too have probably tried to sabotage our wedding, mainly because I want to elope. "Nothing. I'll call and make reservations."

Vince shakes his socks. He always does that after he's worn them for a whole day. "You know we're going to eventually have to talk about your next step."

"What do you mean?"

"Have you decided whether or not to come back to A&Rt?"

I take a long sigh. "I don't know. Let's just get married first."

"It would've been nice to have had you on the team this weekend, Mags. We were only able to get four of the six advertisers back onboard. You would've been able to reel in the other two."

I sit next to him. "Who were you negotiating with?"

"Kevin Lee and Bernard Otter."

"Eek. They're tough."

"You can say that again. I took a chance and put Linda on it this morning."

My smile broadens. "My protégé." I pat Vince on the back. "Good job for finally trusting her enough to give her the dirty work. She'll be able to reel them back in for you. She's sharp."

"Yeah," Vince says with a sigh. "I would rather

have you back, but if you choose another path, then I'll be behind you one hundred percent."

I kiss him quickly. "Thanks, babe. You know, maybe I'll go into the bakery business with Daisy. The last time she was pregnant, she was miserable. This time, she's as happy as a lark. It might have something to do with the mouth-watering French pastries she's been sampling."

Vince puts an arm around me, and I lay my head on his shoulder. "Maggie, you're not a baker."

I let out a long breath. "I know but the time we spent in Hawaii gave me a taste of unmitigated bliss and I'm not ready to lose that feeling."

Vince nods silently and then kisses me tenderly. "Me neither baby, but it's all about balance."

"You're right," I say quietly. "I think I'm afraid of working myself into another frenzy. When it comes to work, I haven't learned the concept of moderation."

He kisses me on the forehead. "I can help you with that."

I lean back slightly. "Thank you, but who's going to help you?"

He chuckles. "Maybe we can help each other."

"Well, that's a recipe for disaster."

Vince nods as he thinks. "Or maybe we could

get some help. Rob is seeing a real good therapist, and the shrinking is definitely working for him. He's like a whole new person."

"I have to agree with that."

"Maybe a therapist can help us find that balance."

I bop my head as I consider the ramifications of seeking counseling. There are no downsides, only an upside. "Okay, let's do it." Suddenly, a bruise on Vince's right foot catches my attention. "What happened to your foot?"

He twists his leg to get a better look. "Didn't I tell you? I almost got hit by a car."

"Yeah, but I didn't know the near collision left you bruised."

Vince shakes his head and throws his hands up. "Damn car sideswiped me while I was out running yesterday. It was like a Lincoln Town Car or limo or something."

"You were running on the streets of New York?"

"No, I wasn't being that kind of dodo."

I chuckle, and he rubs my back. Every time we see an idiot running on the busy streets of the city, we call him or her a dodo. They're literally putting their lives in the hands of some of the most aggressive drivers on the planet—New York cabbies for starters.

"I was crossing the street. I happened to look to my right, and there was this black car coming at me at least fifty miles per hour. So I leapt onto the sidewalk, hit my foot against the gutter, and it knocked my shoe off. The side of my foot smashed into the concrete. It could've been worse." He's massaging his feet like he always does before going for a run.

"Where were you anyway?" I ask.

"On Forty-Eighth and Fifth."

My jaw drops. "Near the A&Rt Building?"

"We were working late."

"Yes, but that's no place to jog, Vince. You know that."

He pecks me on the forehead. "Don't worry, babe. I do it a lot. Almost getting hit once out of a bunch of times is pretty good in New York City."

I'm too exhausted and happy to see him to further debate the dangers of his dodo-like decision to jog near the A&Rt building. Before our three weeks in Hawaii, I hadn't realized Vince was such a daredevil. He's the first to parasail over rough water or bungee jump off a rocky cliff, and he even went skydiving twice. He went surfing every morning, and the few times that I went out to watch him, I found out that he's no slouch. He was good enough to hang in there with the local surfer dudes who own those gigantic waves.

"I see you're about to hit the pavement again," I say.

"Before dinner. I have to get rid of some of this pent-up sexual frustration." He winks.

I sniff and nudge him playfully in the arm. "I know what you mean. Well…" I hop to my feet. "Then I guess I'll see you when you get back."

Vince wraps his arms around my waist and draws me back down to the bed. "But first…"

We kiss. Our limbs entangle. Vince's hands squeeze my breasts, my back, and my waist. Then he slips two hands up under me and grabs two handfuls of my butt cheeks to shove me against his erection. Feeling how ready he is makes me moan and I sink my fingers into his back and caress his scalp as our lips part and he nibbles the side of my neck.

"Vince," I say with a sigh.

"I know." Suddenly, he rolls off the bed. "Going for that run."

I swallow the extra moisture in my mouth as I gawk at his package. "Good idea."

He starts toward the door then stops. "Oh,

wait." He takes his cell phone out of his pocket and taps out a phone number.

I jerk my head back, surprised. "I thought you lost that."

"I did. I bought a temporary one at the airport. Just so Langley could stay in contact with me."

"Oh, like a burner." My cell phone rings, and I scramble toward the closet.

He chuckles. "Like in *The Wire*."

I laugh as I open the closet and sweep my purse off the shelf.

"See you in about forty-five minutes, Carcetti," Vince says, imitating one of the characters.

"As long as you don't juke the stats," I say.

We both laugh as Vince winks at me before leaving.

I open my purse and answer the call. Vince picks up.

"By the way, I forgot to say that I love you," I say.

"I love you too, babe."

I can hear him smile on the other line. "See you soon."

He hums in that way he does when he's full of affection for me. "You bet."

We end the call.

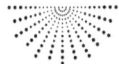

CHAPTER TWO

MAGGIE CONROY

I book us a suite at the Ritz, complete with all the bells and whistles. I can't resist him any longer. Tonight, after dinner, when we arrive at our love nest, I'm officially breaking the pact.

The doorbell rings twice. More of the wedding party is arriving. None of them are my guests. Monroe said she may be able to fly in early, but Hannah and Cleo are flying in on Friday, the day before the wedding. I wasn't planning to have any bridesmaids, but since the sisters insisted, I demanded three of my own friends, plus Angelina, whom they had no problem accepting to the lineup because she's family. On top of that, they seemed impressed with the fact that she's Jacques Blanchard's daughter. But it was like pulling teeth to get them to accept Monroe, Hannah, and Cleo. They wanted eight bridesmaids—all family members only.

"Why only family?" I asked.

"Because that has been our tradition," Lexie had said.

I had to explain that my friends *are* also my family, and if there are bridesmaids, then Monroe, Hannah, and Cleo better be walking down the aisle behind me in their ugly pink dresses. Lexie realized that that was a battle she wasn't going to win, no matter what arsenal of weapons she threw at me. So instead of conceding, she decided to quit. I thought, how not classy and immature of her.

I pack up Vince's and my things in order to make our departure from this house quick and painless. When our suitcases and bags are against the wall, ready to go, I check my watch. An hour has gone by, and dinner starts in less than forty-five minutes. To kill time, I take a shower, which lasts fifteen minutes, tops. I get out, put on a powder-blue knee-length dress with short sleeves and fluff out my short blond hair. Ever since Hannah brought the hairstylist Gianfranco to my apartment in New York to give me a new 'do, I've rarely had bad hair days. I still wear the short but powerfully sexy hairdo. Now that I look A-OK, I check my watch again just to make sure I have the time right. Dinner starts in five minutes. An hour and a half has passed since Vince went for a jog, and he hasn't returned yet.

"Where are you?" I mutter, standing at the door.

I do not want to make another entrance into the dining room by myself. Vince was supposed to be there to take the edge off. Regardless, I take a deep breath, open the door, and slowly start on my way. I'm going to kill Vince when he gets back. But first, we're going to finally make love. I'm sick and tired of being sexually frustrated.

As I step into the dining room, they all turn to acknowledge me for no longer than a snide one second. I gulp nervously and zero in on the one new face that I recognize.

"How are you, Mags?" Robert Tango says.

It takes me a moment to remember that he's

Vince's best man. One night, while we were at dinner with my parents in Hawaii, Vince received a phone call. He excused himself from the table to answer it. Later that night, he told me that it was a reporter from *M&M Magazine*, the world's leading design and photography publication. He agreed to give them an interview for a feature they were writing about a struggling architectural firm that Robert had purchased then transformed in a short period of time. Into the wee hours of the morning, I listened while Vince reminisced about the years he spent being best friends with Robert Tango. Their relationship had all the complications and complexities that exist in Jack and Charlie's relationship.

"Are you really over what happened between Robert and me?" I asked Vince.

"I'm over it," he said.

I studied him with one eye narrowed. "I don't believe you."

Vince turned from staring at the ceiling to look me square in the eyes. "Before you, I never did relationships that well, and before me, neither did you." He stroked my cheek. "When I first saw you all those years ago in high school, I knew we were a lot alike. You were brave enough to wear who you really were on the outside."

I chuckled a little. "You hated me."

"I admired you. Feared you. And actually, I sort of knew I was supposed to love you. That scared the hell out of me, especially since you wanted Rob."

"You were jealous."

He sighed hard. "I *was* jealous. But I also knew that you would ruin our friendship."

"How do you mean?"

Vince covered his eyes with his forearm as if he were about to reveal a deep dark secret. "Because Rob would've fallen in love with you, and I was already in love with you."

I rubbed his arm consolingly. "Babe, you didn't love me. You just had a high school crush on the new girl."

He moved his arm up to peek at me. "I wouldn't expect you to understand, because you're not a guy."

"Ha!" I rolled my eyes at how ridiculous that sounded. Vince nudged me playfully in the side, and I curled my waist, moving away from him. "That tickles," I whined.

We smiled at each other. It was the new us, having fun, reclaiming our inner children, and loving the moments we spent together alone. Then he stroked my cheek again.

"I was afraid of what I felt for you, and that's why I got involved with Emily," he said.

"Promise you won't do that again?"

"I'd never do it again baby. "I've accepted that you're the one, Maggie."

We weaved our legs together and gazed into each other's glassy eyes.

"Me too. You're the only one for me," I said.

From that moment on, we knew nothing in the world could come between us, especially not Robert Tango. Vince felt as if he had to reconnect with his old friend. He felt bad for letting Robert walk away from A&Rt but happy that Robert had made a success out of himself on his own terms. He said he'd always known Robert had it in him. And so, when we agreed to have a traditional wedding, the only best man for Vince was Robert Tango.

I smile broadly at Robert. "Hey, good to see you."

Normally, his eyes travel up and down my figure, but they're not doing that. "Where's Vince?" he asks.

"Out jogging." Another face catches my attention, and I wrinkle my eyebrows, hoping my eyes are deceiving me. "Emily?"

She raises an eyebrow as if she has me stuck in checkmate.

"Humph," Robert says. The tone in his voice makes me force my eyes back on his face.

He's frowning as he thumbs over his shoulder. "I just talked to Vince before I came in. Is he still out there, talking to whoever pulled up in the black car?"

"Huh?" All the words he just spoke are clashing in my head, trying to sort out something that makes sense. "What black car?"

Robert studies my face for a moment. "I'm sure it was nothing."

Before anyone else can say another word, I whip around and dash to the front door. I swing it open and look out across the yard at the end of the drive-way. There's a red car, a white one, and one that looks midnight blue but no black car.

"Hey, what's going on?" Robert asks as he steps up behind me.

There's a sick feeling in the pit of my stomach, and I don't know why. "I don't see a black car," I say.

After a moment, Robert takes out his cell phone. "I'll just call him."

I shake my head. "No. He lost his phone. He's using a disposable phone."

"I know." Robert taps his screen. "Vince told me. I'd been trying to reach him all day."

I hear a sound from afar. At first, I assume it's a cricket, but they make a sharp and fast sound. The sound I hear is slower.

"Do you hear that?" I ask Robert.

Robert shakes his head. "He's not answering."

The noise stops.

My heart is pounding like a drum. "Call him again."

I keep my focus on the end of the driveway, where tall trees rise toward the dark sky on both sides of the cement.

"Okay," Robert says. "It's ringing."

I gasp and squeeze Robert's muscular shoulder. "It's back."

"What's back?"

"The sound. Listen."

Robert drops the phone from his ear and listens. "Shit. I hear it."

We look at each other with wide eyes.

"Hey, what's going on?" someone asks from behind.

Robert and I turn around. It's Carter.

"I don't know," I say then take off toward the sound. "Robert, keep calling," I yell over my shoulder.

I feel as if I'm moving forward rapidly but gaining no ground. Every cell in my body is telling me that there's something to worry about. My feet slap the pavement as I rush past the line of parked cars.

Is Emily really here? The sisters are really trying to rattle me by inviting her for dinner tonight, and their little scheme would've worked if Vince weren't missing. I stop at the end of the driveway, remain still, and open my ears. Robert stops on one side of me and Carter on the other. The chiming is louder.

Carter's arm shoots past me as she points. "It's coming from over there."

We all move in unison. I drop to my hands and knees. The sound is louder. I know I'm not out here alone, but at the moment it feels as if it's just me, the blades of grass that I'm digging through, and the chiming, which suddenly stops. I sigh and then look over at Robert.

He nods once then dials the number again. "It's definitely Vince's phone."

My heart sinks to my belly. Tears fill my eyes. The ringing starts again.

Carter crawls quickly out toward the road. "Got it!" She turns to face us, holding up the cell phone.

My shoulders collapse. I search up and down the dark street. All there is to see are sidewalk, trees, and an empty road. It's as if Vince vanished into thin air.

"What the hell is going on?" Robert mutters.

"Do you know who was in the car?" I ask.

Robert shakes his head. "No."

"Well, what happened? Tell me what you saw." I shake my hands in frustration.

Robert squints thoughtfully. "We'd just finished catching up. He was going to stretch before he came in. I told him I would see him when he gets inside. As soon as I got to the porch, I looked back to find him talking to someone in the backseat of a black car."

"What kind of car?" I ask.

"Looked like a Town Car."

I scrub a hand over my face and sigh, trying to think of anyone we know who drives that kind of car.

"So Vince is missing?" Carter asks.

I study her worried expression then shake my head. "I don't know."

"I'm sure he's okay," Robert says. "Let me make

some calls. He probably just took a quick ride with a friend."

I stare into Robert's eyes. Hopping into a car with friends without telling me doesn't sound at all like Vince.

"He's fine, Mags."

"Is everything okay?" Anne calls.

We turn to look at her standing on the porch.

I raise a hand and put on a fake smile. "Everything's fine!"

"Well, we're having dinner." She sounds as if she's scolding us for leaving the table.

"We'll be inside, Anne," Carter says. "Just give us a minute."

Anne tilts her head. "Where's Vincent?"

Carter and I widen our eyes at each other.

"Something came up. He'll be back," Robert says.

Anne folds her arms. "What came up that was so important that he had to leave without telling me?"

"Something for the company... work," Carter says.

Robert throws his hands up. "You know how Vince is when it comes to business."

I close my eyes and try to get a grip. When I

open my eyes, Anne is watching us. She's too far away for me to get a really good look at her expression, but by her body language, I can tell that she's slightly apprehensive.

"Well... come inside soon. We've already started eating."

Carter smiles. "Okay," she sings.

As soon as Anne goes back into the house, I release the tension in my body.

Carter's eyes shift between Robert and me. "So is this the story we're sticking with, because in less than a minute, Allie is going to walk out that door and demand to know what's going on?"

I sigh, feeling the weight of the world on my shoulders. "I think we should just keep this between us for now."

"Then the story is that Vince stepped away to handle last-minute business?" Robert says.

I nod, holding back my tears. "Yes."

"Then I'll start making some calls," he says. "You two go inside."

Just as Carter anticipated, Allie walks out of the house and asks us what's going on.

"Nothing," Carter says.

She and I avoid giving each other grave looks as we walk toward the house. My footsteps are heavy, and my heart hurts. It's going to take an act of God for me to make it through dinner without breaking down.

CHAPTER THREE

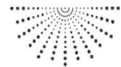

MAGGIE CONROY

I barely make eye contact with the faces sitting around the table, even though they're all paying attention to me.

"Maggie, Lily was going over the plan for Friday's rehearsal dinner."

I look up from my plate to see who said that. It was Madison. She's wearing a sly grin.

"How about we just have dinner at the country club instead of coming back here?" Anne asks.

"Um, I'll have to look into it," Emily says. She's watching me closely, but I wonder why she's even talking.

"Thanks, Lily," Anne says.

I shake my head, flabbergasted. "You're Lily? The wedding planner?"

Emily shows me the phony smile that she used to give me when she was chasing after Vince while pretending she could do my old job. I'm shouting three words in my head, willing them to not explode from my mouth—*what the fuck!*

"So you're the one who arranged my fittings, the cake tasting, and the flowers, and booked the location?" I ask Emily.

"Why yes," she says as if she weren't screwing with me by making sure I had the worst of the worst to choose from.

I fall back in my seat and laugh. I look from Madison to Lexington to Alexandria, and finally to Anne—the woman who is going to be my mother-in-law.

"How could you not tell me?" I ask Anne.

She looks surprised. My body is shaking, and my head is spinning. I've lost all of my carefully crafted composure. I close my eyes and take a deep breath, knowing all eyes are on me. Now I'm positive Anne's been screwing with me alongside her daughters, but it's still in bad taste to call out the mother of the man I love so much on her despicable behavior.

"Sorry…" I anxiously scratch my right temple. "I'm not hungry."

I'm walking so fast that I'm almost running. I clutch my stomach, battling the desire to throw up all the cake samples from this afternoon. When I make it to the bedroom, I get right to work. First things first: I have to get out of this house in order to gain mental clarity. I swipe my phone off the dresser and flip it open. For one second, I allow myself to hope that Vince called while I was downstairs to tell me that he's okay. No such luck.

I call Fast Taxi and ask for a cab in the next fifteen minutes. Just as I end the call, someone knocks on the door.

"Mags, it's me." Robert opens the door.

I search his expression. "Did you locate him?"

The corners of his mouth turn down.

I press my hand over my mouth and close my eyes as a grave feeling washes over me.

"I'll make some more calls."

"Calls to who?"

Robert studies me for a moment. "Some of our old friends that may have taken Vince on a breakout ride."

"A what? Breakaway ride? What's that?" I sound irritated as hell, but I'm a bit relieved and a little peeved at myself. If that's what's happened, then why did I assume the worst? And what is the worst that I'm assuming?

"It's a break-out ride. Our buddy Ben took our buddy Chris out on one before he got married."

I frown harder. "What does this ride entail?"

Robert's eyes shift right before they expand while staring at me.

"What, Robert?" I urge, losing patience.

"A few strip joints and a happy-ending massage."

"What?" I snap. I can hardly believe what he just told me.

He throws up his hands as if to tell me to pipe down. "Listen, Mags, I know Vince, and he's just not one to take that ride." He looks off to think then smashes his lips together as he shakes his head.

"I agree," I say.

"They still could've kidnapped him though."

"Vince doesn't play frat boy, either."

He sighs. "I know."

My phone rings, and I look at the caller ID on the screen. Robert is watching me with his eyebrows raised curiously.

My heart feels as if it's shrinking. "It's not Vince." I answer the call.

It's the cab company. The driver is waiting for

me outside. I tell them I'll be right out. Robert helps me gather my suitcases.

"Let me at least take you to the hotel," he says.

I pick up my suitcase. "Thanks for the offer, but I don't think that'll be wise."

He ruffles his brows as if he has no idea what I'm referring to. "Oh, that…" he finally says.

"They know, Robert. I'm sure of it."

"Who gives a damn? We're not going to repeat the past. I sure as hell learned from that mistake."

I snort, recalling the misery that ensued after screwing Robert Tango. What's funny is that I can hardly remember the act itself. That's the thing about having frivolous sex—it's over just as fast as it starts.

"Didn't we all," I finally say.

"I just don't think you should be alone in the shape you're in."

"I'll be fine." At the door, I stop to give the room a final once-over.

Robert picks up Vince's suitcase and hangs my weekender bag over his shoulder. "I still think you're making a mistake by leaving."

"I don't think so. Vince and I planned on moving to a hotel tonight, after dinner."

"But Vince isn't here."

"I know that," I say snappishly, and take a deep, calming breath. "I mean I know that. When he returns, he'll know where to find me but I can't stay here while he's missing, gone or whatever. It'll drive me crazy."

Suddenly, the door rattles. Robert and I look at each other with hope.

"Come in," I say.

Anne opens the door, and she pays notice to the luggage Robert and I are carrying. "May I come in?" she asks.

"Sure." I step back to let her pass.

She smiles, relieved. "Thank you."

"You're welcome," I mutter. My head's floating in three, maybe four, different directions.

"I want to apologize for not telling you that my daughters hired Emily to be your wedding planner."

I restrain the urge to snort disdainfully. I can't believe she's throwing her daughters under the bus.

"I know it's difficult to believe that I didn't have anything to do with it, but I assure you I had no idea who Lily was until a few days ago."

I part my lips to speak, but Anne holds up a hand to halt me.

"I know that gave me plenty of time to sit down

with you and tell you the truth, but…" She sighs heavily. "I didn't want you to call off the wedding and do what you're doing right now. So I just went along with it, hoping you would too."

My mouth is still open, only now, I'm at a loss for words. "Okay," I finally say. "I believe you."

Anne smashes her hands against her chest. "Thank you so very much. And I mean it. You put the most important day of your life in our hands, and we have been failing miserably." She shakes a finger defiantly. "But no more. I promise you."

I nod acceptingly. "Thank you." I really mean it.

She sighs and studies the luggage in my hand again. "It looks like you're going to leave, but I would love it if you would stay."

"Um…" I examine her earnest expression. I sort of wish she was still acting like the enemy— that way, it would be easier to catch my cab.

"Is Vincent coming back tonight?" she asks.

Robert and I glance at each other. I try to conceal the look I just gave him.

"Um, he's going to meet me at the hotel," I say.

Anne studies me curiously. "And he had to work?"

I can kind of read her thoughts. The more I

think about him having to dash off to work without even coming inside to let anyone know, the odder it sounds.

I put on a fake smile. "Oh no, we just found out he was carried off on a 'farewell to being single' tour by his friends."

She slaps her chest. "Oh, that's a relief. I thought…" She shakes her head. "Well, I'm glad he's okay, but what in the world does a 'farewell to being single' tour consist of?"

"Tons of naughtiness," Robert says. His grin is just as fake as mine.

Anne laughs. "And you're not involved?"

He winks at her. "Not anymore."

She gets a nice little chuckle out of that and tries one more time to sway me to stay. I agree to come over for breakfast tomorrow. She wants me to sit down with her daughters without Emily to straighten out the mess between us.

Robert and I take my luggage downstairs. The chatter at the kitchen table quiets when we pass. I don't even look in their direction. I see that Robert does, and he smiles and winks at them. Stepping onto the porch, I take a deep breath. I finally feel as if I'm making progress.

"Hey, Mags, how about I take you to some places where Vince might be?" Robert asks.

I'm caught off guard by his offer. Ever since I got reacquainted with Robert Tango, many moons after high school, I have never trusted him. I can't say I do now, either. I search for that salacious look in his eyes, but I don't see it. And really, would he risk disassociating himself with Vince for a second time, and this time possibly forever, just to make a pass at me? I am vulnerable. Robert has always done his best work on me whenever I was susceptible to his charm.

"I don't know," I say.

Robert studies me for a moment. "Maggie, I apologize for my past behavior."

I flinch. "What do you mean?"

"Me coming on to you, even though I knew you love Vince and he loves you. You were right—what you said that night when we were in London. I was like a fucking snake in the grass, waiting for my opportunity to pounce on Vince's prized possession. I got you, and that was only temporary. And in the process, I almost lost the one person on this planet I don't want to live without. Vince."

My mouth hangs open in surprise. I don't even

know this Robert Tango that I'm looking at right now, but I trust him. More than that, I need him.

"Okay," I say, choked up.

A slow smile forms on his mouth, and it's not the snaky one I'm used to. "You accept my apology?"

I nod. "And I'll take you up on your offer."

After a brief back and forth, I let Robert pay the cab driver for his time, then we get inside of the midnight-blue Jaguar he's renting. Just before backing out of the driveway, he makes a call. Buzzing resonates from the screen on the dashboard. After the fourth ring, a woman answers. I kind of recognize the voice, but I'm not sure.

"Carter, it's me, Robert."

"Yes?" Her voice is formal.

"Are you still at the table?" he asks.

"Yes," she says in the same tone.

He grins. "And you answered the phone?"

She snickers.

"Is Anne giving you the eyes?"

"Uh-huh."

"Then I'll make this quick. If Vince shows up, could you call me please?"

She pauses. "Um…" I can hear her excuse

herself from the table. After a few more seconds, she asks, "Where are you?"

"I'm taking Maggie around to see if we can find Vince."

She falls silent again. "Oh, okay," she finally says.

There's more awkward silence between them. I feel as if I should say something.

"I'll talk to you later?" Robert says.

"Sure," Carter replies.

He's still grinning. It's strange. "All right. See you soon."

I frown inquisitively.

"Okay. I'll see you," Carter says.

Robert waits for Carter to hang up the phone. That one action of his clues me into something.

"Are you two seeing each other?" I ask.

Robert balls his hand up and puts it over his mouth to clear his throat. "No," he says in a high-pitched voice then clears his throat again. "I mean, no."

I examine his carefully crafted calm demeanor. He's trying too hard, so I know he's lying.

"Well, she's nice and beautiful." I sniff cynically. "Probably the only sane relative in Vince's family."

Robert chuckles. "Probably."

I feel a little like I would be crossing the line if I ask him to tell me more about his relationship with Carter. At least now I understand why she was so gung-ho to help me keep the mystery of the missing groom under wraps. So I choose to abandon the subject of him and Carter.

Robert calls two more of his friends and asks if they've seen Vince tonight. He gives them the third degree, asking the same questions I would have. Each of them asserts that he has no idea where Vince is.

"Brother, we stopped the last steps of freedom caravan after what happened last time," his friend Allen says. "Shit was a disaster. Todd actually fucked the stripper and ran off with her that night. The next time we saw that asshole, he was in a brothel in Reno. Stephanie still blames me for what that fucker did."

"Stephanie's his wife," Robert whispers to me.

I nod.

"Before that, it was John Beattie. After the happy ending at the end of the massage, he decided he didn't want to get married anymore and didn't bother showing up the next day for the wedding."

Robert glances nervously in my direction. "Okay. Thanks."

"So has Vince backed out on his chick? I heard she's a real bitch."

"No, he hasn't. I got to go," Robert says in a rush and taps a button on the steering wheel to end the call. "Ah, Mags—"

I lift a hand to stop him. "Forget about it. I know I have a reputation among Vince's circles."

"Well…" He shrugs. "They're all screwed up anyway. You heard what he said about John and Todd."

I allow myself to chuckle a little. "Yeah, that's crazy."

"Well, that's home folks."

I snicker weakly. "Right."

We spend the next hour going to strip clubs. We even drive to the happy-ending massage parlor. It looks closed for the night, but Robert gets out and knocks on the door. A short, petite lady with black hair opens it. She shakes her head, and Robert waves a thank-you.

As soon as he gets in the car, he takes a deep breath. "Now I'm worried. Very worried."

"Then I take it that he's not in there getting a happy ending," I say.

"Nope."

I close my eyes and let all the strong emotions

war against each other, hoping they'll annihilate each other so that I can think clearly. I sigh hard. "Okay. I need you to take me to the hotel now."

Robert turns to look at me. "Are you sure you should be alone tonight?"

I nod. "Yes. I need to find Vince."

"How?"

I sigh again and shake my head. "I don't know, but I'll figure it out."

Robert scratches the back of his neck anxiously. "I don't know, Mags."

"Just take me to the hotel, Robert. Okay?"

He looks at me as if I'm speaking Dutch.

"Please," I urge him.

After a moment of studying my expression, he nods. "Okay." He starts the car.

Finally, we're mobile again. I like it better when we're moving forward. I won't stop charging forward until Vince is found; that's a promise I make to myself.

ROBERT DROPS ME OFF AT THE RITZ, AND A bellman takes my bags up to my suite as I check in. When they ask if I'll be staying alone, I tell them my fiancé will be joining me. I feel as if I'm lying to myself, and I don't like it.

As soon as I'm in our room, I drag my tired body over to the bed and flop down on the foot of it. At this point, I have only one option.

I take my cell phone out of my purse and place a call. I know it's late and Daisy's pregnant. But my chin starts shaking as the phone rings.

"Hey, Mags, what's going on?" Jack says, sounding half-asleep.

It's clear that I woke him up, but he knows that I would never call him at this hour if I didn't have to.

My eyes water so much that the world around me is blurry. "Vince is missing."

"Vince is missing?" he asks for clarity.

The tears are streaming down my face, and my throat is tight. I want to answer Jack's question, but my mouth is wide open, and there's nothing coming out. When I do let out a sound, it's a deep, guttural cry.

"Help!" I finally shriek. "Please help me, Jack."

The next thing Jack asks is where I am. I tell him, and he says he's on the way.

CHAPTER FOUR

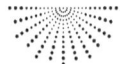

ROBERT TANGO

*I*t's nearly two in the morning when I make it back to Anne's house. I sit in the car for a moment, staring at the front porch. Where in the hell did Vince go? I recall every second of the last conversation we had. It had been way too long since we'd seen each other face-to-face. We gave each other bear hugs. Vince looked good—happy and well rested.

"You're finally going to make it legal with Mags," I said.

"She finally said yes and is sticking to it," Vince replied.

I could see how grateful Vince was to be marrying Maggie Conroy. I always got a sense that Vince thought that if he didn't seal the deal with her that she would get away from him. So there was no way in the world he was just going to run off and disappear into thin air.

I didn't think much of the black car that pulled up after we ended our conversation. It looked like a Lincoln Town Car. I figured whoever was driving it had something to do with the wedding. A lot of people are supposed to show up at the house tonight. I shut my eyes tightly, trying to remember more details about the car.

The windows were tinted. Especially at dusk, the windows made it impossible to see who was driving. Vince was talking to whoever was in the backseat. At one point, Vince folded his arms in front of him, and that sudden move signaled something inside me, but I didn't follow my instincts. I should've walked back to the road and asked if everything was okay. But that's when Allie opened the door and I saw Carter standing behind her, watching me with wide, excited eyes.

My insides turned summersaults, and I had to work to maintain my composure. The last time I heard from Carter, I was reading what she had to say to me in a text message. She sent it on a Sunday after we had spent Saturday together at my house in Napa. After I came back from a run, Carter had split. When I realized she was actually gone, I tried to call her and ask her what the hell happened. The next day, I left my house in Napa and stayed at Jack's house in Russian Hill instead of the hotel I had been living in. Right before I sat down to dinner, Carter had sent a text message. I've read the damn thing so many times that I can remember it verbatim.

"I'm fine. Sorry for the sudden departure. I had fun. I wish you the best."

I tap my fingers on the dashboard as I glare at the house. Carter's in there now. When I dropped Maggie off at the Ritz, I played with the idea of getting a room for myself just so I could avoid the awkwardness of being around Carter, not to mention the discomfort of staving off questions about Vince's whereabouts.

"Where the hell is he?" I say to myself. That is the million-dollar question.

Finally, I get out of the car and walk toward the house. The lights are still on in two of the bedrooms, but one just turned off. The lights to the kitchen and foyer are dim. People must have retired to their rooms for the night already. Oddly enough, I have a key to Anne's house. I practically lived with the Adams family throughout my teenage years.

After I graduated from high school, I tried to give the key back, but Anne insisted that I keep it.

Once I make it to the door, I turn the knob just to make sure it's locked. It's not. Maybe Anne left it open for Vince. I step into the foyer and stand there. What's happening in real life is stranger than fiction. There's no way I can go to sleep, not until I find out exactly what happened to my friend.

"Hey," a voice whispers from the living room.

I turn to see Carter sitting on the edge of the sofa, engulfed by the shadowy atmosphere.

My eyebrows ruffle. I'm surprised to see her. "Hey."

"You didn't find him, did you?" she whispers.

Shaking my head, I walk into the living room to sit beside her. We sit in silence for a moment.

"What do you think could've happened?" Carter asks.

I exhale forcefully as I fall back against the sofa. Is it time to the think the worst? What's the worst that could've happened? "It all narrows down to who was in that black car. We find out who it was, then maybe we can figure out what happened."

"And you didn't see or recognize the driver?" she asks.

I shake my head. "No."

I look at Carter's face. The last time we were this close, we had just made love. She still hasn't told me why she left me high and dry in Napa. I never asked for answers. I would still like to know why she left, but at this point we've both moved on with our lives. She looks good, though—just as captivating as she did the first time I laid eyes on her.

Carter rubs her palms down her pant legs. My staring obviously makes her nervous. I look out the window.

"I'm starting to think the worst," she says.

"Yeah," I say with a sigh, battling the urge to draw her against me to comfort her.

"And what about the wedding?" she asks.

I let myself look into her bright but conflicted eyes. "I don't know. It's all on Maggie at this point."

She frowns. "Yeah, but doesn't she think Anne deserves to know Vince is missing?"

"If it's serious, yes, but we don't know yet."

Carter's shoulders slump. "Right. I get it. Lexie, Allie and Maddie are the last people you want to alarm. They're not real good at handling a crisis." She grunts facetiously. "Plus, they'll only figure out a way to blame Maggie for his disappearance."

"True," I say, knowing exactly what she means.

Carter settles back against the sofa. I wonder if she can feel the sexually charged energy that's flowing between us. Regardless, I'm staying glued to my seat. A time existed when I would've put my hand on Carter's thigh and massaged it as I stared into her eyes, waiting for her to succumb to my seductive powers. But the thought of being the person I used to be leaves a bitter taste in my mouth. I'm four sessions into therapy these days, and I have uncovered some disturbing things about myself. I'm addicted to my bad habits, and the only reason I decided to do something about it is because I finally hit bottom when I had sex with Maggie. That one act nearly ruined the one true relationship in my life—my friendship with Vince. The reason I sought a shrink is because whatever made me act out in the first place was still inside me, waiting for the perfect opportunity to reclaim my life. So even if I do get involved with Carter, I can't trust that I wouldn't end up still being the same uncommitted, sex-starved, drug-starved, and self-loathing jerk I have always been.

"So how is it in DC?" I finally ask.

Carter clears her throat. "Um, right, the Metropolis firm is great," she says gleefully.

"It was Stuart Beatty who poached you from me, wasn't it?"

Carter looks at me with wide eyes. I was just joking with her, but I would love to say it again, just to see that sexy expression on her face.

"Um, well, he didn't *poach* me. I applied for the job way before you took over Kennedy Creative."

I wink at her. "It's okay, Carter. I heard you're doing great things out there in DC."

Her posture stiffens. "You have?"

"Yes, I have."

She focuses her inquisitive gaze on me.

"What? You don't think you're doing great things?" I ask.

She shakes her head spastically. "No. That's not it."

"Then what is it?"

"Um…" She turns to look at me and opens her mouth to speak but then closes it.

"What is it?" I urge. I'm on the edge of my seat. I don't know what I'm hoping she'll say, but that look on her face is making me as horny as hell. I can't deny the robust sexual attraction I have for her. Strictly by accident, I acted on it once. Rather than doing it again, I'd like to wait and see if she and I can get something serious, something real going. I like Carter that much.

Her eyes are wide and as curious as a doe's eyes. "It's just that... um. You were checking on me?"

I take a deep breath in order to get a grip. I want to kiss her, but I know I can't. "Yeah. I did."

"Oh." She doesn't sound upset.

My heart is beating a mile a minute. I can't stop my lips from moving toward hers. We hold firm eye contact. I'm trembling. Shit, I just might do this right here and right now—fuck her until I'm running on fumes. Then the light clicks on. Carter and I scramble to put distance between us.

"Why are you guys still up?" Allie asks. She's standing by the light switch, frowning as if she thinks she may have caught us fucking or something. She's wearing a fuzzy pink robe, and her hair is pulled into a high ponytail.

"We were just talking," Carter says.

Allie glances down at my crotch. I'm as hard as steel, so I cross my legs to hide it.

"About what?" Allie asks.

"Architecture stuff," Carter says before I can think of a response.

Allie hesitates as if she doesn't really want to accept the answer. "So has Vince made it back yet?"

"He won't be back for a while," I say.

"Humph." Allie grimaces. "He just left without letting us know." She shakes her head while rolling her eyes. "Typical Vince."

I already know Allie isn't going to leave Carter and me alone again, and I'm sort of bummed about it. She looks so soft sitting there. I want to be inside her, right now. I stand. "He'll probably call me in the morning. I'll let you know what he says."

"And Maggie just left?" Allie says as though Maggie's leaving is the greatest sin against humanity.

Carter and I widen our eyes at each other.

"So…" I say in a concluding tone. "I'm going to go to bed." I shoot a finger at Carter. "It's good seeing you again."

Carter clears her throat and springs to her feet. "Likewise."

I smirk, feeling flirtatious. "*Likewise* you're glad to see me, or *likewise* you're going to bed?"

"Both," she says.

I'm seized by her alluring grin. Is she coming on to me? I would still love to spread her out and ravish her, but the thought still scares me. I don't want to end up hurting her, or any woman.

So I smile resolutely at Carter and Allie. "See you in the morning."

I go straight to my guest room and sit on the side of the bed to take off my shoes. Suddenly, a memory comes to me. I did notice one aspect of the black car—the emblem on the front. It was shaped like a crest. The colors were indecipherable, but it was definitely a Cadillac. I'm certain of it. I don't know how that can help, but at least it's a start. I resolve to call Maggie in the morning to tell her. She's probably asleep by now. She looked exhausted when I last left her.

CHAPTER FIVE

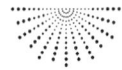

MAGGIE CONROY

*T*he room phone rings once. I blink. The room is full of light because I forgot to close the curtains, and my head is heavy. The phone rings again, and I flip over and reach out to the nightstand to answer it.

"Hello?" I say, my voice hoarse. I squeeze my eyes shut. The daylight is making my head hurt more.

"Good morning, Miss Conroy, you have a guest. A Mr. Jack Lord. Could I please send him up?" The woman's voice is too cheery.

I wish I could be as happy as she is. My dilemma rushes back into me like a strong wind. Vince is missing, still.

"Yes, please send him up," I say before hanging up.

I'm still in yesterday's clothes, and I don't even remember falling asleep. I was sitting against the headboard, trying to think of where Vince might be. I made a mental list of people to call at 6:00 a.m. sharp—Langley, Rachael Pope, Don Limmerick, Jessie Caldwell, Donna Mason, Leigh Dosier, and Harvey Little. They were all part of the meeting Vince held on Friday and Saturday in New York. I would've reached out to them before I fell asleep, but I didn't want to alarm anyone.

I wrap myself in the white bathrobe hanging in the closet. It's pretty chilly in the room—I didn't turn down the air conditioner before falling asleep. There's a knock on the door. I finish tying up the robe and run to answer my callers.

I open the door and clutch my chest. "Jack. Daisy," I barely say past my tight throat. Just seeing their faces makes me tear up again.

Jack hugs me, and finally, I feel like everything is going to be okay. Then Daisy and I hug, and I get a double dose of that same feeling. Her presence is definitely an unexpected and pleasant surprise. The last time she was pregnant, Jack didn't want her flying on airplanes and nearly pitched a fit whenever she had to leave the house.

"How are you, Mags?" she asks, rubbing my back.

"I'm hanging in there—I think," I say, scrubbing the tears off my cheek.

"Here, I'll get you some tissues." Daisy trots off to the half bathroom. For a fraction of a second I notice that Daisy is sporting a brand new sexy pixie cut that has taken her beauty to an unimaginable level.

"So…" Jack's expression is all business. "I made some calls last night."

I bob my head. "To who?"

"To the entire management, and some business associates that Vince and I had to get tough with a few weeks ago."

I wait for Jack to elaborate; instead, he clamps his lips together and intensifies his frown. He's thinking. At least he's called everyone on my list. Upper management, as well as Langley, knows this is our wedding weekend. At A&Rt Media, news like that spreads like wildfire. If Jack is asking where Vince is, then at least they won't suspect he's a runaway groom or something. Such a rumor would burn like a struck match through the company, from LA all the way to Sidney, Australia.

Daisy comes back with three neatly pulled tissues. "Here you go, Maggie."

I take the tissues. "Thank you." I wipe my eyes and blow my nose.

"Maggie," Jack says in a serious voice.

"Yes."

He looks me straight in the eyes. "Don't worry. If Vince is still on the planet, then we'll find him."

I hold my breath while nodding continuously. I believe him.

"Here's what we're going to go. Daisy is going to Vince's mother's house. You were planning your wedding with his sisters?"

My mouth can't speak, so I nod.

"Daisy will take your place."

I look at her with wide eyes. She smiles reassuringly. I'm pretty sure Daisy can handle Allie, Maddie, and perhaps Lexie—it's just that I love her too much to put her in my shoes with them.

"Are you sure? They can cause quite a lot of stress." I look down at her stomach.

She rubs her pregnant belly. "Don't worry. I can manage," she says.

Jack winks at her. "She's in tip-top shape."

I nod while I sigh, glad to hear it.

"So here's the deal, Mags," Jack says. "You're coming with me. That way, it looks as if the three of us—you, Vince, and I—are engaged in A&Rt business."

"Yes. That's smart. Thank you," I say, relieved.

There's another knock on the door. I look from Jack to Daisy with wide eyes.

I grab my heart in hopes that what I feel is real. "Vince." I run to the door and open it. My heart sinks. "Robert?"

The corners of his eyes turn down sympathetically. "Sorry, Maggie. I told the front desk you were expecting me."

I let Robert in, and we gather in the sitting area but no one sits. The first thing he tells us is that he remembers the type of car he saw before Vince disappeared.

"A Cadillac?" Jack repeats.

"Yeah. The kind that's used for shuttling."

Jack nods while wrinkling his eyebrows. "That's a good start. It's likely that whoever was in that car wasn't local."

"The car was a rental?" Robert says.

"Perhaps," Jacks says then frowns dubiously. He sighs. "We should get started. I don't want this to get too far ahead of us—timing is everything."

We decide that's a good idea. Robert drives Daisy back to Anne's house for breakfast. She'll be staying at Jack's parents' house, which Jack has renovated to the max since Aunt Carlotta and Uncle Charles died so many years ago. He doesn't want her there alone, which is typical Jack, so Robert agrees to stay with her. There was a time I would have cringed at the thought of Daisy alone in a house with a scoundrel like Robert Tango, but I've noticed a marked difference in him.

I SIT ON THE SOFA ALONE WHILE JACK, DAISY, AND Robert go downstairs to transfer Daisy's things to Robert's car. Every second that Vince is gone feels like an eternity. I rack my brain, trying to figure out who would just snatch Vince out of thin air. Normally, I'm really good at figuring out mysteries. The fact that I can't come up with one viable suspect drives me crazy.

Wait. Could it have been Emily? She and Vince's sisters have gone through great lengths to sabotage our wedding. Maybe the sister's kidnapped him just to keep us apart.

The key-code makes a sound, and the door opens. I turn to see Jack taking deliberate steps in my direction. I shoot to my feet and my suspicions about Emily and Vince's sisters pour out of my mouth like a tsunami of blame.

Jack waves a hand dismissively. "No. They're clear."

"How do you know?"

He stops in front of me. "I spoke to Vince while he was in New York this past weekend. He told me the women were giving you a hard time so he wanted to hurry and get back. So I had them all checked out during our flight to Denver. None of them exhibit suspicious or incriminating behavior."

My shoulders as I hug myself while staring at him with solemn eyes.

He squeezes my shoulder. "Have a seat, Maggie."

I sit back down and look up at him with solemn eyes. My hopes have been thwarted.

Jack sits next to me. "Have no doubt that we will find Vince, but I need you to follow my gut and not your own—got it?"

I nod as if he's merely stating the obvious. But

his dire tone has me more alarmed than I was at first. "What do you think happened to him?"

He studies my face and then takes the intensity out of his own expression. "I don't know, but people don't just vanish into thin air. Something happened to them. But you and I are in a unique position to find Vince because of all the tools I have at my disposal."

"What tools?"

"That's one of the questions I need for you not to ask. Whatever happened to Vince—if he ran off with someone else—"

"He didn't."

Jack presses his lips together in a patronizing smile. "I know."

I don't believe him. I think he *does* think it's possible. But he wasn't with us in Hawaii. Vince and I are just as in love and needing of each other as he and Daisy are.

I shake my head resolutely. "Vince would never do that to me and that's a fact."

He pats my leg. "I believe you. Now let's get the show on the road." He leaps to his feet.

I let his energy pervade me as I get up and grab my purse off the dresser.

"You won't be needing that," Jack says. He's already standing at the door.

"But I need my ID and my…"

"Leave it."

I frown while studying his expression. He's serious. "Okay." I gently push my purse against the wall.

Jack holds the door for me as I leave the room. My hands are sweaty and my heart is jumpy. I have no idea what's supposed to happen next.

"Can I ask you where we're going?" I say as we walk down the hallway.

We stop at the elevator, and Jack pushes the down button. "To the airport."

"We're leaving town?" I ask, shocked.

The elevator doors slide open, and we step inside.

Jack presses *L* for lobby. "I'm positive Vince isn't still in Colorado."

I furrow my brows. "How do you know?"

"I'll show you once we get to where we're going."

I'm about to demand he tell me where that is, then I remember his directives. I still wonder why he insists on all the secrecy. Come to think of it,

Jack is always secretive. I think he's more comfortable operating that way.

I scratch my ear as anxiety brews throughout my body. I don't have to be in control, but I still want to at least be on equal footing with Jack in this situation. "And that's to the airport?"

"Yes," Jack says.

"And I can't ask you where we're going?"

He folds his hands together in front of him. "You already have."

"But you haven't answered."

"No I have not."

I roll my eyes while groaning.

Jack puts his hands on my shoulders and looks me straight in the eyes. "Maggie. I'm letting you in because I trust you can handle it. Don't make me regret my decision. You're going to have to trust me more than you have ever had. Okay?"

I take a long sigh and hang my head. The truth is Jack has never let me down—ever. I'm pretty sure he's not going to start now.

"Okay," I say. "Your way, not mine."

CHAPTER SIX

ROBERT TANGO

*M*y hands are steady as I clutch the steering wheel. I try to appear cool, calm and collected but inside, I'm as nervous as hell. I'm alone with Jack Lord's wife? No man in the world would leave a woman as beautiful as she is in my care, let alone trust me to stay in his house alone with her. But just by her demeanor, I can tell that Daisy is not the kind of woman who would cross those lines, or at least I don't get that vibe from her.

Daisy remains quiet as I drive down the highway. She has one hand on her pregnant stomach as she stares out the window. I shift nervously in my seat.

"So is this your first time in Colorado?" I ask.

I glance at her just in time to see her face me. She's a rare beauty.

"No," she says with a delicate smile.

That was a stupid question. Of course it isn't her first time here. I'm suddenly hot so I pull at my collar.

"I heard your bakery is pretty happening," I say, trying to recover from my previous thoughtless question.

Her smile turns broader. "Yeah, we're doing pretty well."

I wait for her to say more. Damn if she isn't a woman of few words. "It's a French bakery, right?"

"Right."

"And your specialty is beignets?"

"They'll melt in your mouth," she sings proudly.

I toss my head back to laugh. I hadn't expected her to say that. "And why is that?"

She goes on to enlighten me on what's so good about her beignets then divulges her "secret" recipe step by step, adding that she learned how to make them from a French woman who lives at her father's chateau in Bordeaux.

I find Mrs. Lord very interesting. She and Jack brought the French woman who taught her how to make perfect pastries to the States and set her up in the cottage of Jack's vineyard in Montecito. The place looks just like her cottage in France, but within three days she was ready for them to put her on an airplane and fly her back to France.

"This is not too much," Daisy says with a French accent. "But what she really meant was that it *was* too much." Daisy chuckles and throws her hands up. "There was nothing around but grapevines, olive groves, and a horse stable. She didn't even have to go to the restaurant to cook!"

I glance at Daisy long enough to watch her look off thoughtfully.

She smiles slightly. "I guess she missed her family and friends. So Belmont and I ended up spending two months in Bordeaux while Ines taught me everything she knows about baking mouthwatering pastries." After a brief pause, she chuckles. "She was like a pint-sized drill sergeant. She would slap my hand when I put a pinch too much flour in the batter. But she would reward me with a wet kiss on the cheek when I did something right. It was the most strange, rewarding and intense training I had ever undergone."

"Seems as though her method worked."

"It certainly did!"

I smile. "Says your cash register."

Daisy's grin grows wider as she shrugs her eyebrows in agreement.

I toss my head back and laugh harder.

Regardless of the heaviness that had broken out surrounding Vince's disappearance, I'm smiling from ear to ear. I want to ask if this is how she landed Jack Lord, by being charming as hell, but instead, I laugh some more at another story she tells me about pet-sitting a naughty little "purse dog" for one of her friends. The dog pissed on all her walls, gnawed on her furniture and jumped into the swimming pool.

"Belmont had to dive in and save him! Poor thing was so spoiled that he didn't know how to dogpaddle."

I'm still laughing when I stop in front of Vince's mother's house. Four cars are parked in the drive.

Daisy's slight smile fades. "There are a lot of people here."

"Anne prefers a full house, and she damn well makes sure she always has one," I say.

Daisy turns to look at me inquisitively. "Interesting."

I shift in my seat. It's as though she can read deep into the comment I made.

"Just so we're clear: Vince is with Maggie and

Belmont. He and Maggie apologize for having to leave so suddenly, but the show will go on Saturday afternoon at five o'clock as planned."

I nod. "Got it."

Daisy looks back at the house with a frown. "Good."

WHEN WE WALK INSIDE, EVERYONE HAS ALREADY gathered for breakfast. At least thirteen people are sitting around the long table. I recognize just about everyone at first sight. There's one face that I've seen before but can't quite place. She gives me a strange smirk then stares at Daisy. Carter is watching me as I watch the familiar woman. But then she looks away as soon as I look at her.

Daisy smiles pleasantly as all eyes fall on her. She has the biggest presence in the room. I'm sure she's used to being gawked at, which is why it's no surprise that she's not rattled.

I clear my throat. "This is Daisy Lord, Jack Lord's wife."

"Good morning," Daisy says, in complete control. She places a hand over her heart. "Maggie will be gone for a few days, along with

Vince and my husband. A serious emergency came up."

"What—" Anne begins.

Daisy takes her hand off her chest and gently raises it to put her at ease. "It's nothing dire, only work. The company is going through a difficult time right now, and they really need Maggie's expertise to dig them out of this hole."

Lexie snorts bitterly. "I'm sorry, but what's her expertise?"

The green light switches on. Daisy will be facing Vince's sisters' bitchery starting right now.

Daisy looks Lexie straight in the eyes without flinching. "Maggie is a superior marketing expert, one of the best in the world."

Lexie sneers for a moment, but then she straightens her face and sits back in her seat without a rebuttal. I'm shocked by how quickly Lexie backed down from an opportunity to belittle Maggie. She's been spreading rumors about Maggie being a gold digger, even though not only is Maggie is successful in her own right but she's got the Lord billions at her disposal. Both Jack and Charlie will stop whatever they're doing to run and help her whenever she needs them.

Anne shoots to her feet. "Well, we're glad to

have you as our guest, Mrs. Lord. I'm afraid we're out of rooms but—"

"That's fine. I'm staying at our home here in town. It's not far," Daisy says.

Anne touches her chest. "Oh, Carlotta and Charles' manor."

"Yes."

"I heard Jack did a lot of work to it."

Daisy maintains her gracious smile. "Yes, he did."

"Well, I guess that's that." By the look on Anne's face, she really doesn't like the fact that she wouldn't have the opportunity to make space for another guest, especially Jack Lord's wife. Anne points to an empty chair. "Well, why don't you have a seat over there?"

"Thank you," Daisy says, maintaining her pleasant demeanor.

"Robert, why don't you sit between Carter and Allie?"

I really want to trade seats with Daisy. She's sitting next to Maggie's copper-haired friend. She hasn't stopped smirking since Daisy and I arrived, and her name still eludes me. We met once at one of Maggie's birthday parties. I remember admiring her long legs and beautiful eyes. I thought she was hot, but I didn't want to hit on her or anything. Something about her screamed, "Stay away" and still does. So I can resist Maggie's friend, but smelling the sweet floral scent of Carter's perfume or shampoo and feeling her energy would make it harder to resist Carter.

Finally, I take a seat. "Morning, ladies."

"Up early, I see," Allie says. Her tone always insinuates that I've been out doing something wrong. However, I have decades of experience in handling Allie.

I wink at her. "Then that means I caught the worm."

She looks off and mumbles, "Apparently, you went out and caught Mrs. Lord."

I don't let her get away with that one. Daisy doesn't deserve her scandalous insinuation. "What are you trying to say, Allie?"

She sniffs and turns away to whisper something to the poor schlub she's supposed to be marrying.

I shake my head and turn to Carter.

Carter rolls her eyes and mouths, "Ignore her."

I smile, thankful for the obvious advice. "How did you sleep last night?"

Carter massages her neck. "On a pullout sofa in the den."

Suddenly, Anne claps her hands to get everyone's attention. Carter and I are forced to rip our gazes away from each other.

"Well"—Anne looks around the table—"the bride isn't here. That's what happens when your son marries a busy woman." She smiles at Daisy.

Daisy maintains an indifferent expression.

Anne ruffles her eyebrows a little but continues. "But I promised Maggie that from this point on, we will thank Emily for her services, but we will no longer be using them."

Maggie's friend snorts cynically. "Emily? Emily Calhoun or Callahan or something? Isn't that the bitch who tried to steal Vince from her?"

Everyone at the table looks at her in awe. Now I remember her name—it's Monroe. She's notorious for being irreverent.

"Well, I'm here to help move the wedding plans along," Daisy says on cue.

"We're glad to have you," Anne says, seemingly thankful to Daisy for taking the sting out of Monroe's comment. "This afternoon, we're finalizing the cake and the venue's decorations."

"Perfect," Daisy says.

Anne smiles at her. I've seen that smile many

times before. Daisy has won her over—Anne will be putty in Mrs. Lord's hands.

"I still don't understand why we have to let Emily go," Maddie says.

"You wouldn't," Monroe says.

My eyes expand in disbelief. Monroe just will not let up.

"Excuse me?" Maddie snarls, part insulted and part incensed.

Monroe shakes her finger at her. "You and your sisters have been making this shit hard for Maggie from the beginning. Now"—she points at me —"you're Robert Tango, aren't you?"

I'm tongue-tied for a moment. "Um, sure…"

Daisy puts her hand on Monroe's shoulder and looks her dead in the eyes. "Could we not do this now, please?"

Monroe's face goes through various expressions before she settles on an eyebrow shrug and a concil-iatory, "Whatever."

As breakfast ensues, everyone who isn't involved in the wedding planning is forced to sit and listen to the sisters duke it out with Monroe over decorating the ranch for the wedding ceremony and reception. It's sort of entertaining to watch Monroe not back down from Lexie and Maddie's intimidating tactics, which are composed of whining, raising their voices, and asking questions in a snippy and sarcastic tone.

"Vince likes silver. He wants it draped over the top of the benches," Lexie says.

Monroe whips her face around to glare at Daisy. Her expression asks, "Can you believe this?"

She turns her grimace back on Lexie. "Well, Maggie sometimes likes the rustic look, which I gather is the reason why she let you put her wedding in a fucking barn in the first place. But she doesn't like tacky, and silver covers over wooden benches are tacky."

Lexie rears back and expands her eyes as though she's been slapped in the face.

"Hey, let's watch our language," Kevin, Lexie's husband, chimes in.

Monroe scowls at him as if he just dropped in from outer space and is speaking a language she doesn't care to learn. She guides her finger between Vince's sisters and mom. "And about the catering and cake and shit like that—you know very well that Vince couldn't give a flying fuck about it. What you have been doing is using his name to give my friend a hard time. Well, that's *over*. I want to see every fucking thing from the cake to the rice you're going to throw when Maggie and Vince run the fuck away from this cluster-fuck."

"Monroe!" Daisy says sternly.

Monroe sits up straight. Her fury had made her lean forward. Daisy and Monroe glare at each other. For a second, I think Mrs. Lord and this crazy Monroe are finally going to turn on each other. That would make Lexie, Maddie, and Allie happy. I'm almost compelled to do something about it.

"Monroe is right," Daisy says, shocking the hell out of me.

I quickly turn to Carter, who has also been following the interesting discussion. We smirk at each other.

"I'm here—we're here—to make sure Maggie and Vince get what they want out of *their* special day. It's not *our* special day." Daisy smiles tightly at Monroe. "And we will make sure that happens. But we will all work together and keep cool heads." She raises her hand. "I'm in agreement, are you?" She stares at Monroe.

After a moment, Monroe sighs and rolls her eyes. "Yes, as long as they stop the shit."

Both women set their inquisitive expressions on

the sisters. Maddie and Lexie do that thing where they communicate with their eyes.

To my surprise, Allie throws up her hand. "I'm in."

I'm used to her going along with Lexie and Maddie's program.

Carter raises her hand. "I'm here to help, so I'm in too."

I raise my hand. "Hell, I'm here to chauffeur the pregnant lady around, so I'm also in."

I wink at Daisy, and she smiles charmingly. It takes me a moment to look away from her angelic face. I'm positive that, to some degree, I've fallen for Mrs. Lord—not in a romantic way, though. I'm in love with the fact that someone so strong yet delicate, so very beautiful, and obviously clever and inviting is going to be part of my world for at least four more days.

Maddie's and Lexie's jaws drop as they glare at Allie as though she's Benedict Arnold.

Anne raises her hand. "Of course I'm in." She points to Maddie and Lexie. "And so are they." She turns her Stepford smile on them. "Or you can choose to be out. I think we can handle it between the *six* of us."

Finally, Maddie says she's in, but Lexie, the most

stubborn of the three, says she'll stay out of it. Finally, the wedding drama ends, and my nervousness about sitting next to Carter returns.

Carter groans while circling her shoulders.

"Are you okay?" I ask.

She puts down her fork and massages her neck. "I'm thinking about staying in a hotel. Hell, why not? I can afford it now that I'm making the big bucks."

I sniff a chuckle. "So is that why you left RT Creative? I didn't pay you enough?"

She rolls her eyes as she massages her neck deeper. "No, that's not it."

I study her. Lots of shit goes through my mind. Can I invite her to stay at Daisy's? The thought of a beautiful woman like her staying in a hotel downtown alone drives me crazy. I want her near.

I shift anxiously in my seat. "How about you stay with us? I'm sure Daisy won't mind." Before Carter can respond, I call Daisy.

"Yes?" Daisy says, lifting her eyebrows.

"Do you mind if Carter stays with us?"

"Not at all." She smiles invitingly at Carter.

"I'm staying with you too," Monroe declares.

Allie turns her snarl on Carter. "You're not going anywhere."

Carter smiles at Daisy, completely ignoring Allie. "Thank you, Daisy. I truly appreciate it. I can use a good night's sleep."

Of course the fact that two guests are leaving Anne's house is the start of another long conversation, which begins with Anne making sure no one else will choose to leave the confines of her hospitable domain. Then the conversation turns into building more mother-in-law quarters in the backyard, and Lexie uses that opportunity to pry into Daisy and Jack's affairs by asking if Jack will be interested in doing the work.

"Isn't he a contractor?" Lexie asks.

Daisy just smiles graciously and says, "You would have to ask him that yourself."

"You don't know whether or not your husband is a contractor?" Lexie persists.

Daisy offers her that smile again as she calmly puts the eggs on her fork into her mouth and chews as if she didn't hear a peep from Lexie.

Monroe snickers. "Well, okay then—I guess you have your answer to that question." She laughs louder. I think Daisy has just made a fan of Monroe —and hell, me too.

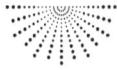

CHAPTER SEVEN

MAGGIE CONROY

"*R*obert gave me this," Jack says.

We're on his private airplane inside a cabin, standing in front of a long table that has a computer control center on one side. I find the whole setup jarring. What does Jack need with all of these computers and screens?

I turn my attention back to Jack. He's already reminded me a number of times that I am not to ask questions—so I don't.

"That's Vince's temporary phone," I say.

"Yes." He holds it up. "You see this hairline crack running down the middle?"

I squint to see it. "Yeah, I do."

"It's not there by accident. Watch."

Jack puts the phone into something that looks

like a microwave. He taps on a keypad connected to the machine, and it turns on. My lips are parted in awe as I watch a sheet of fluorescent light flow over the device. The computer system turns on.

"What's happening?" I ask Jack, figuring that's a question he can answer.

"The saturated light is extracting cells off the phone and making a digital copy of them."

I study Jack with furrowed eyebrows. "I thought you were in commercial real estate."

He sniffs a chuckle. "I am."

"Then what's all this?"

Jack studies me with one eye narrowed. "You're good, Mags, but that's a question I still can't answer."

There's a loud beep.

"Over here," Jack says.

I follow him to a flat-paneled monitor. He powers it on and works the keys. Robert's face comes up. It's a mug shot, and the side text says that he was arrested for drunk and disorderly conduct in 2013. A picture of me from the A&Rt directory comes up as well. Vince's photo follows, then there's one of a burly man with thick jaws, a bald head, and hard eyes.

"Bingo!" Jack starts reading his rap sheet, which

is two pages long. "Assault with a deadly weapon, attempted murder, vehicular manslaughter..." Jack snorts. "This guy's a pawn."

"What do you mean?"

He glances at me then continues to grimace at the man's image. "Douglas Randall's rap sheet is not his own."

My frown intensifies.

"He's a man for hire," Jack clarifies.

"How can you tell that by reading his rap sheet?"

"It's pretty heavy for him not to be behind bars. He never got convicted for any of it. And here's why." He pulls up another list, which details court dates, attorneys, and judges. "Every one of them is dirty."

"How do you know that?"

"I know," he says confidently.

I'm standing here, looking at Jack, but I feel as if I'm spiraling down a rabbit hole. I shake my puzzled head. "What are you? Some kind of secret agent or something?"

He types on the keyboard. "I told you, Mags. I can't answer that question. I've already shown you too much, but I'm choosing to do whatever it takes to find Vince, and the first forty-eight hours are crucial to finding him alive and well."

I clutch my stomach. A sinking feeling rolls around inside it. I'm tempted to ask the one question I've been dreading. But the longer I stand behind Jack as he works on his control center, the closer the question inches toward the tip of my tongue.

"Pennsylvania," Jack says. He rushes over to the phone on the wall and picks up the receiver.

He winks at me as he waits a second or two for someone to pick up. "How far are we from Teterboro?" He's nodding. "Good." He pauses. "How soon?" He pauses. "Then redirect." After a beat, he hangs up.

"We're going to New York?" I ask. My heart is beating a mile a minute.

"Yes." Jack places another call. This time, he places it on speaker. After two rings, the caller answers.

"Jack?"

I already recognize the voice.

"Gray, Maggie's here with me," Jack says.

"Maggie? Hey, Maggie."

It takes me a moment to process Gray Lansing's 360-degree turn from being surprised that I'm here to being cordial about it. He's done work for me for Mo&Ma. I always figured he was an undercover super hacker by day and a trust fund baby by night. I figured he hacked and spied to get his kicks and he just happened to be good at it. But here he is part of Jack's clandestine operation.

"Hi, Gray," I say.

"Jack, I pulled the shots you were looking for, but after you sent me a query request for Douglas Randall, I figured this is all you'll need."

Suddenly, images of a bald, burly man in a black jacket fill the screen.

"Got them," Jack says.

He and I study the images from top to bottom. In one of them Douglas Randall is walking out of the car rental office, looking over his shoulder. In another shot, he and two other slimy-looking men get into a black car with tinted windows, which is the same kind of car Robert saw Vince standing next to. One of the guys slide behind the wheel, and the other two get into the backseat with Douglas.

"Did you pull the details on the two others?" Jack asks.

"Sending them through right now," Gray says.

That sick feeling in the pit of my stomach intensifies, and I have to throw up, but I make myself keep it in. There are shots of the car driving down the highway, passing a gas station that I've seen many times while taking the road to Anne's house.

"They're in Anne's neighborhood," I say.

"The neighbors' surveillance systems captured them."

I shake my head. This is all insane. "I mean, is any of this legal?"

Jack looks at me with a blank expression. I read his face loud and clear—he's not going to answer.

I clutch my stomach. The queasiness is too much to bear.

"I'll be back," I say before running to the lavatory. Once I'm there, I lift the lid of the toilet and stand over it, waiting for something to happen. I feel nauseated, but I haven't had a meal since lunch yesterday. I remain still and take another assessment of my body.

"Gosh, Maggie," I whisper. I ball up my fists and press them over my eyes. I'm gripped by a powerful feeling of sorrow and loss.

A sound surrounds me, and my lips are moving, but the words are coming from outside of myself. I hear my voice repeating, "What are you going do?"

I drop my fists from my eyes. "Get a grip." If I

fall apart, then I'll be no good to anybody, let alone myself. I pull a bunch of tissues from the holder in the wall and wipe the tears from my eyes and cheeks. Then I blow my nose and stare at myself in the mirror. My sad and lonely image reminds me that this is real. There's no waking up from this nightmare. This. Is. Real. Vince is missing. Three thugs took him—one with a rap sheet longer than my leg. And now, by use of some incredible and extraordinary means, Jack is going to find him. Choosing to hold on to that hope, I throw the tissue away and walk back to the cabin.

Jack is leaning across the control center, reading the screen. He turns to look at me. "Are you better?"

I nod. "Um-hum."

"All right." He faces the screen again. "We'll be landing in thirty minutes. I'm not going to put you in any dangerous situations, but I'll need you to drive me where I tell you to take us."

I nod again, but realizing he can't see me, I say, "Okay." My throat is tight, and my body is jittery.

"When was the last time you ate?"

I hug myself. "Um, yesterday."

Jack nods. "Okay, well, there's a meal waiting for you in the main cabin. Go eat; try to relax." He stands up straight and smiles at me. His optimism already makes me feel a little better, at least well enough to follow his instruction.

I put my hand on Jack's shoulder as I pass him.

He puts his hand over mine. "Don't worry, Maggie. Heads are going to roll for this. You better believe it."

I look deep into his eyes. I'm jolted by something within Jack that I have never seen before. I believe him. I just saw a man equally, if not more, dangerous to the one we're out to find.

As Jack said, our plane touches down in Teterboro thirty minutes later. I'm still alone in the main cabin as the plane taxis across the runway. I chose not to return to Jack's high-tech room because at the moment, it's a little overwhelming. I'm just ready to get out there and find Vince. I'll feel better once we're finally on the ground, getting this done and over with.

The plane stops. Jack walks out from the back. He's wearing black pants and a black T-shirt with utility boots. With his bulging biceps and broad chest, Jack's presence fills the cabin. It appears to me that he's ready to fight. However, that reality is not computing. Jack isn't a fighter. He's a fixer—a caring man who uses his money and contacts, not his fists, to get what he needs done. At least that's what I thought.

He barely looks me in the eyes as he sweeps past me. "Get ready to disembark."

I nod, but my head feels as though it isn't attached to my neck. I unlatch my seat belt.

Jack knocks on the door to the cockpit, and the co-pilot opens the door. He goes inside just as the flight attendants come out from a small room adjacent to Jack's private room. The woman and man barely acknowledge me when they pass. They work with the ground crew to open the door.

Jack steps out of the cockpit. "Let's go, Maggie."

I rise to my feet. My legs are trembling, and I'm unable to control it. Jack is the picture of confidence and competence. It's as if he's been in this situation a million times before. He stands by the doorway, waiting for me to take the ramp first. That's the Jack I know—still chivalrous.

He smiles firmly at me as I pass him. I pause, waiting for another assurance that everything is going to be fine, but at this point, he probably has no more guarantees to offer. I let my shaky legs walk me down the ramp.

A sleek gray luxury coupe with tinted windows is waiting for us near the bottom of the ramp. As agreed, I take the wheel, and Jack gets in the passenger seat. He puts the buds, which are connected to a compact computer tablet, in his ears.

"Follow the road out," he says.

I squint at the clock on the dashboard. It's seven minutes until noon but feels so much later than that. However, that's a good thing because we still have the whole day ahead of us. I start the car and take the road to the exit, which is easy to find. I've flown out of and into Teterboro enough on one of Jack's, Charlie's, or Vince's private planes.

"Get on the I-95 North," he says.

"Okay." I glance at Jack, who's staring straight ahead. That feeling from earlier washes over me. My cousin Jack has left the house. Who is the guy I'm sitting next to? Something tells me I'm about to find out.

I'VE ALREADY TAKEN I-95 TO HIGHWAY 1, AND NOW

we're in Trenton, New Jersey, heading toward Pennsylvania. I shift uncomfortably in my seat. I have a great urge to ask Jack where in the world we are going.

I cross the Delaware River. However, Jack hasn't changed that intense look on his face since I started driving, and frankly, I'm a little intimidated by it. Clearly, he's the one in charge; I'm just along for the ride.

"No one can know that I'm using what's available to me for this personal mission of ours," he says out of the blue.

I quickly turn to face him. "I won't say anything." He looks me in the eyes, and before I know it, the question drops out of my mouth. "Do you think he's alive?"

"Make the next right," he says.

Anticipation hangs in the air as I wait for an answer. I make the next right and glance expectantly at Jack.

"I think so," Jack finally says.

"Why do you think so?"

"Because I feel it in my gut."

I narrow my eyes to slits. I'm not sure if I want to cry, sigh with relief, or yell at him for placating me.

"I don't believe you," I say calmly. Tears rush to my eyes. I win the battle to hold them back.

Jack sighs sympathetically. "In times like this, don't think about the future. Focus on the here and now, because that's where we're the strongest."

I take a minute to grasp what he's saying. He's right. The present is all we can control at the moment.

"Make the next left," he says.

In about three hundred feet, I turn into a residential neighborhood.

"From this point on, don't look at the addresses," he says.

I frown. I wonder why, but I don't ask. Instead, I let Jack guide me down a maze of streets until he tells me to park in front of a house.

I turn to my right and observe a white house that needs a paint job and new roof. "Is that where he lives?"

He pulls a messenger bag from under the seat. "Where who lives?"

"Douglas Randall?"

He glances at the house. "No. Stay put. Lock the doors and don't open them for anyone but me."

He doesn't wait for me to respond to his directives before hopping out of the car and heading down the street behind me. I study him through the rearview mirror. The bag is hanging on his shoulder as he strolls casually, as though he's a resident who walks this street every day. However, I lose sight of him when he turns down the next block.

I press the lock button, and the doors click. I sit as still as I can be. At this point, all I can do is wait. I close my eyes, take three deep breaths, and work on remaining in the present.

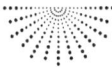

CHAPTER EIGHT

ROBERT TANGO

I had no idea agreeing to chauffeur Daisy around would be so much work. I'm in the bakery with six other women. Monroe is talking —she's always the one talking.

"What the hell is this?" she says, looking down at a piece of paper in front of her.

The woman behind the counter looks at Monroe as if she's trying to contain how annoyed she is by her. "It's the cake."

Monroe continuously stabs the page with her finger. "I know, but why do I see chocolate mousse and chocolate cake? Get rid of that shit."

"No. Maggie agreed to it," Maddie whines.

"Maggie abhors chocolate with her cake. It gives her a fucking rash. Therefore, she nor her guests will be forced to eat it on *her* wedding day." She pushes the sheet back toward the woman behind the counter. "Make it all white with buttercream filling and frosting."

Maddie slides the paper back toward her. "No. Keep the bottom tier chocolate."

Monroe slides it by to the woman. "Nope. White."

Maddie frowns as if she just sucked on a lemon. "You can't come in here and change the order."

"I did and I will." Monroe nods firmly at the woman behind the counter.

"Sarah…" Maddie says pleadingly.

Monroe sneers. "Listen, *Sarah*…" She side-eyes Maddie. "The bride's with me"—she points her thumb at Daisy—"and her. So if you want to deliver a cake to the Adams wedding, then you should really change that order to what I said. White cake. Buttercream frosting, and that's it."

Anne claps her hands. "Okay," she says diplomatically.

Daisy puts a hand on Monroe's shoulder and flashes her winning smile at Sarah. "What she said—no chocolate. So we're getting the five-tier cake…"

I tune them out. Instead, I focus on Carter, who

is standing beside Allie. I'm looking at her, but I can't stop trying to figure out what happened to Vince. As far as I know, Vince isn't a gambler or anything, so he wouldn't have gotten involved with loan sharks. Maybe it was a business deal gone south. Maybe Jack knew more about Vince's disappearance than he let on. They're still business partners.

Something's replaying over and over in my head. When Jack asked for Vince's temporary phone, and I handed it to him, he made a point to grip it from the sides. Why was he being extra careful? Did he think the phone was evidence? Regardless, I probably won't feel fully settled until I could look Vince in the eyes again and see that he's okay. I feel as though I'm in the wrong place right now. Instead of driving Mrs. Lord around, along with Monroe, who's probably certifiable, I should be with Jack, doing whatever it takes to find Vince.

"Thank you," Monroe says and whips herself around to put her back to the woman behind the counter.

Although I wasn't really paying them much attention, I heard enough to discern that Monroe got her way. Now they're approving the cake design.

Carter turns just in time to catch me staring at

her again. She smirks. By the look in her eyes, I can tell she's not impressed by all the drama surrounding the wedding cake. I smile back at her, and Allie notices. Allie has always had a thing for me. However, she and I are like oil and water, or even better, a human body and sulfuric acid—she's the sulfuric acid.

Allie whispers something to Carter, who rolls her eyes. Carter walks toward me, and I wonder what she wants to say to me.

Anne claps her hands. "Now that that's settled, let's head to the ranch."

In one fell swoop, all the women turn to walk in my direction. I'm disappointed. Whatever conversation she wanted to have with me, I wanted to have it.

Like the newfound gentleman I discovered inside me, I open the door for the ladies.

Allie wraps her arm around Carter's arm as they pass. "Glad that's over with," she says to Carter.

I feel butterflies in my stomach when Carter walks by. Maybe I shouldn't try to stay away from her. I want her. I want her bad.

❄️

Like the drive to the bakery, I carry Daisy and Monroe in my car, and Anne, Carter, and Allie ride with Maddie. I can imagine how they're tearing Monroe down in that car. Of course Monroe deserves it—she's been nothing short of a bitch.

"Can you believe them?" Monroe complains.

"Yeah," Daisy says with a sigh. "It seems they've been giving Maggie hell."

Monroe falls back against her seat. "Thank you. I didn't think you got it."

"Oh, I got it. But you just keep yelling and insulting them, and I'll remain the voice of reason. It's been working."

Monroe lets out a loud laugh then hugs Daisy's seat. Her face is right in the space between the driver and passenger seats. "Get the hell out of here —you mean to tell me that you've been playing them all along?"

Daisy turns to face her, smirking. "Like a fiddle."

Monroe balls her fists and sings a happy note. "No wonder you were able to land Jack Lord. You're fucking amazing." She kisses Daisy on the cheek.

I glance at Daisy just in time to see her look at me with a squeamish look.

"Well, thank you, I guess," Daisy says.

"Now can you put your seat belt on?" I say, watching Monroe through the rearview mirror.

"Oh, don't get your boxers in a bunch." She sits back in her seat. "Or briefs. Or do you go commando?"

I stifle a chuckle. Despite her being a bit crass, I find Monroe to be amusing.

"Anyway," she says, "what going on between you and Vince's cousin, Carter?"

I shift uncomfortably in my seat. "I don't know what you're talking about?"

"I see... Deny, deny, deny? Don't pretend as if nothing is going on between the two of you, Tango. Neither one of you can keep your eyes off each other."

"There's nothing—"

"And let me tell you, that's not easy to do when I'm in the room." She pauses. "Or Daisy over there. Even PG, she's the hottest piece in the room."

Daisy grunts and rolls her eyes.

"And see, that makes it even worse because she downplays it, which makes her even hotter. But anyway, this is what I want to know, Tango." Monroe pauses, watching my frown with an amused look on her face. "So when did you two fuck? Because I'm positive you fucked."

"Monroe?" Daisy scolds.

I swallow nervously. The fact that I had sex with Carter is the last thing I want to get back to Vince. Whenever I need a sharp dose of reality, I recall the conversation between Maggie and Mavis, my former executive assistant. I'm easily able to stand in the same shoes I stood in on the morning I was banging a woman in my supply closet.

We actually get more done when he's not here.

He's such a game player.

I think he looks at your ass and pussy like he's a starving hyena.

To him, women are pussies not people.

And finally, *I think his greatest ambition is to be trapped in a porno.*

They said a lot more than that, but those are the things that haunt me like the ghost of Robert's past. I'm quite sure Vince thinks the same of me, and Vince would probably cut off my balls if he thought I was donking his cousin.

"That's okay, Daisy. I can answer," I say.

In the rearview mirror, I make eye contact with Monroe. She's smirking, proud of herself.

"Carter and I have never fucked," I say in a convincing tone of voice.

She folds her arms. "I'm calling bullshit on that."

I shrug. "Believe what you will." I play out my indifference by looking straight ahead, unfazed.

"Okay then," Monroe says after a long moment of silence. "I'll buy it—I guess. If you're lying, then you're better at it than I am."

I glance at her in the mirror, and she's studying me with tapered eyes. She's an inquisitive one, but I've been a master liar for a long time.

"Good," Daisy says with a sigh of relief. "Glad that's over with."

"Me too," I say with a chuckle.

"And for the record, Robert, Carter would be lucky to have you. You're a good guy, and that's a fact," Daisy says as if she instinctually knows she should negate the script in my head.

"Hey!" Monroe says as the car swerves.

"Oh shit!" I steady the car.

"Don't kill us," Monroe says calmly.

"Sorry about that."

"Just keep your eyes on the fucking tail end of Allie's or Lexie's or whatever the hell her name is rear bumper."

"It's Maddie," I say.

"Oh… anyway, getting back to what Daisy just said—she's right."

"Right about what?"

"You're a good guy, Tango. I'm just giving you hell because I'm bored."

I smile. It's good to receive two affirmations that I'm not seen as the oversexed asshole Maggie and Mavis made me out to be. And hell, I might be this close to believing it myself. *This close.*

"Thanks," I say to Monroe.

She gives me the thumbs-up.

CHAPTER NINE

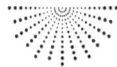

MAGGIE CONROY

J check my wristwatch. Jack's been gone for one hour and thirteen minutes. What if the big, burly guy got the jump on him and now he needs help?

I shift in my seat as I panic. Jack instructed me to not open the door for anyone except him and told me to stay put. I twist my mouth nervously. I still think I should get out and search for Jack. One big problem is I have no idea where he went. We're in a standard suburban neighborhood. It shouldn't be that hard to distinguish which house belongs to a hardened criminal, but then again, I'm pretty sure just about everyone in this neighborhood has an angel face but a closet full of skeletons.

I would call him if I had my cell phone, but Jack

made me leave it at the hotel. If I were a fingernail biter, I would be chomping on them right now. I grab the door handle. Do I, or don't I?

I let go. "Get control of yourself," I tell myself.

I close my eyes and take one deep breath, then another.

Knock, knock, knock.

I quickly open my eyes. I grab my heart in relief as I see Jack standing outside the door. I hit the unlock button. He gets inside and stuffs the shoulder bag back under the seat. I'm shocked by a small bloody gash under his right eye.

"What happened?"

He looks straight ahead. "Drive, Maggie, and don't speed away from the curb."

I'm stuck in awe as he opens the glove compartment and takes out a white packet.

Jack turns his hard glare on me. "I said drive, now."

He's never used that tone with me, but it works. I turn on the engine and drive off.

He rips open the packet. "Make a left at the next corner, go all the way down to the end of the street, and make a right."

I nod spastically. "Okay, but Jack, did you get into a fight?"

He takes a square bandage out of the packet and puts it on the gash under his eye. "I know who hired him."

"Geesh, but did you have to fight to find out?"

"Maggie," he says, scolding me.

"What? I know you made me promise not to ask any questions, but this is ridiculous, Jack!" I make the car turns he asked me to make.

"Take us back to Teterboro. We're going to Las Vegas."

I frown, disenchanted. "Vegas? That's a long way away."

He peels the bandage off his abrasion and some sort of silicone sealant has closed the gash. "That's where Peter Oslo is."

I wrinkle my eyebrows as I think. That name rings a bell. "Wait. Isn't he Vince's old business partner?"

Jack stuffs the gauze in a compartment. It must be some sort of trash chute.

"Yes," he says.

My heart beats frantically as I try to keep the steering wheel steady.

"Calm down, Mags. This is one reason why I instructed you not to ask questions. I need you to do one thing for me. Drive, and do it with preciseness —got it?"

I have more questions to ask about Peter Oslo, but Jack is right. I'm shaken now, and the more I know, the more unstable I become.

Jack must've won the tussle—he came back in one piece, along with new information. Peter Oslo hired that big, burly guy in the video.

"So you fought that Douglas Randall guy?"

Jack admonishes me with his eyes again.

"That shouldn't be a top-secret answer. Either you did or didn't."

"Yes, I fought him."

I grunt, intrigued. My brain tries to conjure images of Jack in a fistfight with such a meaty and muscular guy. Jack is not a small man, but he's not a brute. Then I remember the bag he took from under the seat. Did he have weapons inside of it? I bet he at least has a gun.

"Did you shoot him?" I ask quickly. It's a tactic I've used with clients. The brain's first inclination is to tell the truth. So a quick question usually merits a quick answer.

"No," he says. It worked.

Jack sniffs and shakes his head. "You're too clever, Mags."

I smirk as another comes to me, and before I ask it, I run down everything that I know about my cousin. I heard rumors that he used to be a gigolo in Las Vegas. I know a lot about human behavior, and Jack pleasuring women for money didn't seem likely. And do men go from gigolos to multi-billionaires in less than ten years? I know he received a hefty inheritance, but Lord & Lord Steele was operating in the red when Jack took over the company after his parents' death. There were even rumors swirling that Uncle Charles and Aunt Carlotta's airplane was sabotaged so his partners could get the money Uncle Charles owed them. By the time Jack and Charlie got their piece of the pie, billions had turned into millions. But now Jack has more billions than his father had. And I can't pinpoint exactly what he does for a living. Commercial real estate? Multimedia? Banking? Investments? He knows a lot of people and knows how to get impossible strings pulled—Pete Oslo being one of those strings. Oslo was going to make Vince marry his daughter or make it very difficult for Vince and Robert to ever have the majority ownership in the company they built from scratch. Maybe that's why he kidnapped Vince. Payback. But that's not what I want to ask Jack—at least not first.

I drive up Highway 1, staring straight ahead. I know this question is ridiculous, but not implausible.

"So, Jack?"

"Yes, Maggie."

I don't let his tetchy tone detour me. "Are you an agent?"

He looks at me as if that's the most ridiculous thing in the world. And frankly, after that, I don't need him to say anything else. I read behavior for a living, and I've read his.

Jack opens the cargo container between our seats and takes out the mini-computer he has been using. I'm pretty sharp myself, and I think it's time for Jack to use my instincts instead of just having me here to chauffeur him around.

I glance at Jack. "Contacting Gray?"

His mouth tightens like he's annoyed by my question. "Yes, I am."

"You want him to tap into all of Peter Oslo's lines of communication, right?"

Jack's eyes remain on his device as he continues to type. About ten seconds later, I conclude that he's not going to answer.

"Gray's done that for Mo&Ma a number of times, so…"

"Maggie, no," Jack finally says.

"No to what?"

"I'm not going to make you a more integral part of this."

I figure this is not the time to impose my will. After all, I'm in a delicate situation. It still feels as if I'm caught between a Stanley Kubrick film and a nightmare. Jack is the only solid foundation I have to hold on to right now. He's always had his way of getting shit done; I figure that's exactly what he's doing now. There's no need for me to get in the way of progress—at least not at the moment.

"Okay," I say.

Jack snorts as if he doesn't believe me.

Regardless, I speed up, figuring the sooner we get to the airport, the sooner we'll find Vince.

THREE HOURS LATER, WE'RE BACK ON THE AIRPLANE. Jack makes sure I eat again, even though I'm not hungry. But at least this time, he eats with me.

I ask Jack how Daisy has been doing with the pregnancy.

"She's well. She's eating enough. I thought she wouldn't be able to get much rest, being that she's running the bakery, but she's really able to rely on her staff."

"Good," I say enthusiastically.

I'm extremely glad to hear Daisy is not miserable during this pregnancy. The first time around, she was always swollen, bloated, cramping, and exhausted—and yet she kept on pushing herself. However, I have another goal in mind. I'm hoping to make Jack relaxed enough to give me more information about what he plans to do when we arrive in Las Vegas.

"How often do you leave her alone when you fly off for business?"

He shifts in his seat. "Not often."

"Do you take her with you?"

Jack glares at me as if he knows exactly what I'm doing.

I grunt in defeat. "Jack, I just want to know more about what's going on here. I mean, you go and fight a guy, and now we know Vince's ex-business partner hired him. I mean, what are we going to do when we arrive in Las Vegas?"

Jack sighs, clearly exasperated. "You know why I brought you?"

"To be your driver," I say gruffly then immediately want to take it back.

"You're too much of a doer to sit idly at home and wait," he says, seemingly unaffected by my tone.

"Well that's true."

"I also knew you could handle all of this."

"Yes. I can."

"The way you exposed Yvette Maynard and the Reece Corporation for setting me up—that was impressive." He shifts in his seat and rubs his chin. "When this is over and all is back to normal, I have a proposition for you."

I take a quick glance at him. "Do you think all will return to normal?"

"I have to say, at the moment, I think so."

The tension falls out of my shoulders as I sigh relieved. "Okay then, what's the proposition?"

"How about we table this conversation for now?"

I turn to glance at him again and he winks at me. I can let it drop. It sounds as though he wants to discuss a career option and now is certainly not the time to make that kind of decision—even if I'm curious as hell to hear what Jack has to offer. First I just want to find Vince and then marry him. However, the good thing is that I have Jack exactly where I want him.

"I just want to know one thing," I say.

He looks at me suspiciously. "What?"

"You must have a guess why Peter Oslo would kidnap Vince."

Jack sighs again. I realize I have an advantage: he hates being sharp with me. I'm pretty sure it's already tearing him up inside. And I hate making him too uncomfortable, so I tread lightly.

"Oslo is one of those guys who hates to lose."

A rush of relief flows through me. Now I'm getting somewhere. I narrow an eye inquisitively. "So when he sold you his shares in A&Rt Media, it was because he lost?"

Jack cracks a smile, shaking his head.

I'm sure he sees me as a gnat that just won't go away. I try to mask a victorious smile. "So what did you have on him?"

Jack tilts his head to assess me. He's done that a number of times already. I keep the look of expectation in my eyes.

"I'll be back." He goes into his Bat Cave on the airplane, and I take another bite of the chicken potpie that I've already let get too cold.

In a flash, Jack returns with another computer tablet. He seems to have an endless supply of them.

After pulling something up on the screen, he hands me the device. I clutch it, but he doesn't let go.

I raise my eyebrows. "What?"

"This doesn't mean I'm going to tell you everything you want to know."

I nod like an eager puppy dog. I really want to see what's on the screen.

Jack releases the device, but the screen is dark.

"There's nothing on it," I say.

"Press your thumb on the identification button at the bottom."

I tilt my head toward Jack. "You have my fingerprints programed on this?"

Jack snickers. "The answer to that is no. I set it in a mode for you to view exactly what I want you to view."

"But why does it need my thumbprint?"

"So the device knows you're not me."

I press my thumb to the button at the bottom of the screen. The screen turns on immediately, showing photos of a man who looks to be in his sixties engaging in sexual acts with very young prostitutes. The longer I study the images, the farther my jaw drops. "Is this Peter Oslo?"

"Yes."

I shake my head. "So you blackmailed him with these photos?"

"You've heard of the CVCP?" he says.

"Yeah. The ultra-right-wing purist group who fund projects of interest."

Jack nods. "Peter Oslo is on the board of directors."

Suddenly, I'm struck by illumination. "But you had those photos before you used them to make him sell his interest in A&Rt Media. Why?"

Jack smirks as he studies me. "That's a very good question you asked, Maggie. However, I will tell you that my interest in Peter Oslo has nothing to do with his hypocrisy."

Suddenly, Jack's seat buzzes. Before I can ask what's going on, he races back to the Bat Cave. I'm on his heels. Once we're in the small room full of electronic equipment, Jack works a number of dials.

"Gray?" Jack says as he glances at me.

He's not only let me in the room, but he also let me listen to this call. I nod, thankful for the access he's giving me.

"Somehow, Randall was able to get a message to Oslo. He knows you're looking for him, so now Oslo's on the run."

Jack curses under his breath. An intense frown hijacks his face. He's looking slightly to the left, which means he's visualizing his memories. I wonder how he left this Randall guy. By the looks of the situation, he left the man alive but incapacitated.

"So where's he going?" Jack asks.

"He's going to New York, but before he boarded the flight, he had a conversation with Dale Finley," Gray says.

"And what was said?"

"He was wondering why you're on his tail."

Jack grunts thoughtfully. "He would know why if he had anything to do with Vince's disappearance."

"That's what I was thinking," Gray says.

"Me too," I say.

Jack frowns at me as if he's giving me that look as an afterthought.

He turns his scowl back to his contraption. "He's flying into Teterboro?"

"Yes he is," Gray says.

"That means he's running scared. He has people to keep him safe in New York."

"So what are you going to do?" I ask.

Jack gives me that look again—the one that says

he's trying to figure out how much disclosure to grant me.

"Who are his pilots?" Jack asks.

"Lionel Armstrong and Ben Taylor."

Jack sits down in front of the console. "Maggie, could you please return to the cabin?"

I'm about to whine, but I think better of it. Back in my hotel in Denver, I agreed to not ask questions if he brought me with him. I've broken our agreement so many times, and he hasn't put me on the first flight back to Denver, at least not yet. But if I keep pressing my luck, he probably will.

I go quietly back to the cabin. As soon as I take my seat, the flight attendant comes out to ask if I would like a snack or beverage. I take advantage of the fancy menu and order a vanilla latte.

As I wait for my caffeine fix, I try to keep my nerves in check. Still, I can't get Peter Oslo out of my head. We're missing a variable. Peter doesn't know anything about Vince's disappearance, yet the thug, Douglas Randall, warned him about Jack. I wonder how dangerous Jack is. Apparently, scary men run and hide from him. I also remember Vince telling me that Gabrielle, his former fiancée and Peter's daughter, had a strange sort of incestuous relationship with her father.

Suddenly, a thought hits me. I leap out of my seat and run to Jack's private room. I try to turn the knob, but the door is locked, so I knock.

"Would you like me to keep your latte warm?" the flight attendant asks.

I jump, startled. "Um, yes please."

The door opens. There's a stark contrast between the dim and the cabin.

I check over my shoulder to make sure the flight attendant is out of sight. She hasn't made her way to the room where the food is prepared.

"Can I come in please?" I say, sounding eager.

Jack studies me shrewdly then finally steps back.

I close the door behind me. "Gabrielle. She's the one behind Vince's disappearance."

Jack rubs his top lip contemplatively. "That's very good, Mags. Follow me."

I have pep in my step as I follow him back to the console. I feel as if I've finally proven my worth. Plus, the thought of Vince's crazy ex-fiancée snatching him sits better with me than a bitter businessman kidnapping him. At least Vince has the edge. He's smart enough to play Gabrielle for as long as he needs in order to escape her clutches. And I'm sure he knows I'm looking for him.

I grab my heart and take a breath of relief as

Jack continues talking to the pilots of Peter Oslo's aircraft. I close my eyes for a moment, hoping Vince feels me with him. A tingle ignites in my body, and I skip a breath.

"He's alive." I grip the back of a chair to control the emotion surging through me. "He's definitely alive."

Jack and I stare into each other's eyes, and he nods. He may be placating me again, but I don't care. I know I'm right.

CHAPTER TEN

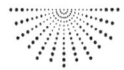

ROBERT TANGO

I'm watching the women duke it out over the details. We're inside an elaborate barn at Reinhardt Ranch. I guess this is where they're going to hold the ceremony. Monroe can't stop shaking her head as she examines the haystacks and the dry wooden benches flanking the aisle.

"Who the fuck picked this place to have a wedding? I know for sure Maggie didn't."

"You're the one who said Maggie preferred the rustic look," Maddie says.

Monroe shoots her a look that could take out an army. "No way…" She looks at Daisy. "We have three days to turn this shit around."

"I'm not letting you do this. This is Vincent's favorite place."

"To fucking ride a horse! Not have a wedding!"

Maddie whips her face toward Anne. "Mom, say something."

So far, Daisy has been winning these battles, but her lips are still parted in awe. Even I have to concede that this venue is a dump. Allie's slated to get married next. I bet she would never say *I do* in this shit-shack.

I turn and catch Carter watching me, which makes me aware that I'm smirking. I wink at her, and she cracks a tiny smile.

"So what's going on between you and Carter?" Allie says.

I jump. She's right on my left shoulder. I didn't even see her standing there.

"Didn't you ask that already?"

"And you lied."

"If you think I'm lying, then why do you keep asking?"

She's about to answer that when my phone rings in my pocket. I raise a finger, secure my phone, and hurry out of the barn-house junkyard.

My shoulders slump in disappointment when I check out the name on the screen. I was hoping it was Jack calling to say Vince has been found.

"Hi, Zoe," I say, answering my assistant's call.

"I know you're away this week, and I really, really, *really* didn't want to call you, but I didn't know what to do."

I walk across the dusty ground on my way to the parking lot. "It's okay. What's going on?" I look down at my shoes. They're covered in dirt. I try to stomp as much of it off as I can before I get into the car. Then I settle in behind the steering wheel. "What's going on?"

"Just thought I'd let you know that we're very close to not submitting our bid for the Atlantic Metropolitan Library Project. It's supposed to be submitted by eight tomorrow morning."

"It hasn't been submitted yet?"

"No," she says sharply.

I can sense how stressed she is.

"Why not?"

"Because of Grace."

Sighing, I rub the inside corners of my eyes. Of course Grace is the reason for the delay. I gave her full operating control of Kennedy Creative Interior Designs, a subsidiary of RT Creative, but that hasn't made her more of a team player. We have a running joke around the office about Grace's hiring choices. We call it the three-week cliff. No one she's hired has lasted for more than three weeks. In two months, she's gone through six employees. I let it go on for far too long because I've been busy trying to make a name for RT Creative in architecture firms around the nation, but it's about time to get Kennedy Creative Interior Designs in line.

Unfortunately, today is not the time. I offered Grace the opportunity to add an interior design plan to the proposal to make our bid look stronger and to help get the subsidiary higher off the ground.

I'm still rubbing my eyes as I try to think. "Have you received the proposal from the architectural team?"

"Yes." I can tell by Zoe's tone that she's relieved I asked that question.

All of a sudden, there's a knock on the passenger-side window, and I quickly look over to see Anne waving.

I wave her inside the car. "Then submit it," I say to Zoe.

She sighs with relief. "Thank you."

Anne gets into the passenger seat, and I cradle my phone closer to my face. "No, thank you for staying on top of this. I'll see you on Monday, Zoe."

"You're welcome, and sure, see you on Monday," she says.

We hang up.

"What's really going on with Vince?" Anne asks before I can open my mouth to speak.

"Nothing."

"Robert...." She tilts her head to study me shrewdly.

"He's really okay, Anne. I promise you."

"Then why are you scratching the tip of your nose?"

Shit. I clutch the steering wheel with both hands. "Because it itches."

Anne wiggles a finger. "You're lying to me," she sings.

I stare right into her green eyes. Looking at her is almost like watching Vince. Vince looks more like his mother than Simon, his father, who more than likely will not show up for the ceremony. Simon's estranged from Anne because he left her for another woman. His daughters stopped talking to him because of it. But Vince hadn't cut ties with his father. He has a meal or a drink with Simon every now and then. Sometimes I join them. He's a good guy, whose only crime was falling in love with another woman. Regardless, lying to the people I care about used to be easier.

"Vince *is* in New York," I say.

Anne rubs an eyelid like she's frustrated. "Is he hurt?"

"No," I say as if I really believe it. The truth is I don't know, but I hope not.

She shakes her head as she gazes straight out the window. "I just don't know."

I watch her, wishing I could tell her the truth—but I can't. She would call the police and tell everyone Vince was kidnapped by treacherous killers, then his story would be headlining the evening news tonight at eight. "I know how all this sounds, but this situation is one of those rare deals."

"Well…" She sighs resignedly. "He did have to fly back to New York on Friday to handle some work issue. I didn't understand it then, either. I tried to make him see that this wedding is really important."

"Right," I say, figuring I should let her continue driving down the road she's going.

"It's just…" Her frown intensifies.

"Listen, Anne, I'm sure Vince will call you as soon as he can."

"Has he contacted you?"

I shake my head. "Net yet. But, you know, when Vince is in the middle of the fire, he gets single-minded."

"Yes, that is true. He's always been that way, even when he was a little boy. He'd spend hours building those model building sets."

I snicker. "I remember that."

We're silent, and I'm hoping like hell Anne's ready to end this conversation.

"Okay... I better get back in there before the girls tear each other into pieces."

"Right," I say with a nervous laugh.

Anne searches my expression again, and I try to look as innocent as a first-semester Catholic school-girl. Finally, she opens the door and gets out. I watch her until she scurries back into the barn.

I lay my seat back, rest my head, and close my eyes until they're done. I've had enough of bickering women for the day. I don't get to rest long— soon Daisy and Monroe are back in the car, talking about leaving early the next morning to find another venue for the wedding. Monroe tells me that I don't have to worry about tagging along— she's going to drive one of the cars at the house. I don't protest. I'm over this wedding business. I would rather sit around and twiddle my thumbs as I wait for Jack to find Vince.

I struggle to stay alert as I drive to the Belcaro Park neighborhood, which is about twenty minutes from Anne's house. However, I wake right up as soon as we pull into the driveway of Jack's residence, which looks like a redbrick Victorian castle. The guy has exquisite architectural taste, that's for sure.

I drive slowly up the driveway, which cuts through the emerald lawn. "Nice house," I say, noticing how thick and green the trees are.

Daisy smiles. "Belmont's mother and father used to live here. He's done a lot of work on it in the past two years."

"Right," I say, remembering the Lords did live in this neighborhood. It's strange to remember that Charlie and Jack are also from Denver, and we all attended the same high school. I used to see Jack a lot on campus, and he always looked busy. Vince and I used to joke about him acting more like a teacher than a student. He even parked his Beamer in the faculty parking lot, and the principal let him do it. I tried that once, and my F-150 got towed. Though I'd always felt like asking why Jack got special treatment, I didn't. Hell, I probably believed he deserved it.

I stop in front of the door and help Daisy and Monroe with their luggage. Once inside, I'm struck by the smell of new furniture and new construction.

The interior is designed like a contemporary English country home with grand but clean armoires and large sofas, chairs, and tables, and modern chandeliers hang from high ceilings. I take Daisy's luggage to her bedroom, which is an enormous but comfortable space. She hands me a garage door opener and directs me to the garage at the back of the house. Before I store my car for the evening, I carry my things to one of the second-floor guest rooms at the south end of the house, far away from the room Monroe's sleeping in.

After I fall on the bed a few times to test the mattress, which is like sleeping on a piece of heaven, I zip back to my car and drive to the garage. I park next to a burgundy Range Rover. A BMW Roadster is parked on the other side of the SUV. I'm surprised those are all the cars Jack owns. He has one for the snow and one for warm days like today, but I can tell neither has been driven in a while.

I reenter the house through a door in the garage. I mosey down a brick hallway and past an empty kennel until I reach an opened door. As soon as I walk in, I'm struck by the smell of wine that's being cooked with food and tasty spices. I pass the kitchen, where a woman in a chef's coat and hat is at the stove; smoke is rising from a pan as she stirs the ingredients inside it.

I pop my head into the kitchen. "Excuse me."

The chef turns around. She's in her forties and pretty attractive. "Yes, sir?"

I fight the urge to flirt. "Um, what time is dinner?"

She checks her watch. "It'll be late tonight, per Daisy's request, but I just sent servers up to your rooms with cheese and cracker plates for snacks. Dinner's at seven."

I want to clap my hands and shout, "Hot damn!" I can afford to live like Jack Lord, but I probably never will. Still, since I'm here, I intend to take full advantage of the fruits of his labor.

I thank the cook and return to my room. I put on a comfortable pair of sweatpants and a fresh T-shirt. I'm not sure if Carter's lodging here or not. I guess I'll find out at some point.

Next, I look for the cheese platter. It's sitting on the desk near the window beside my messenger bag. There's even a glass each of white and red wine. I sniff, impressed. Jack sure knows how to hire the right people.

Thinking of Jack, I call him to get an update on the hunt for Vince. The call goes straight to voicemail. I leave a message, asking him to call as soon as he can. I go back to the desk to get my red wine and pull my computer out of my bag. The scene in the backyard catches my attention. The sun is dropping behind a line of tall and thick poplar trees that surround a private lake with a walking bridge across it. The entire back-yard resembles a lavish English garden, but the bulbous trees, trimmed shrubs, and colorful flowers are climate appropriate. Right in the middle of the paradise is a fluffy lawn surrounding a circular courtyard with an in-ground fire pit in the center.

Since the sun is going down it's a tad bit cooler out, probably about sixty-two or -three degrees. Daisy and Monroe are sitting around a blaze, in white wood chaise chairs, snacking on cheese, cold cuts, crackers, and fruit. Monroe is drinking wine, and Daisy has a glass of water in her hand. For one second, I consider staying inside, but the company of two attractive women is far better than sitting here, checking email and calling Grace to chew her out for missing the deadline.

I slide into my slip-ons, skip down the steps, and turn down a series of hallways until I come across the door to the backyard. On the ground, the backyard is far more impressive than the view from my window. It's expansive—about four acres.

"Some backyard," I say, walking up to the two women.

They both turn to look at me.

"I thought you had enough estrogen for the day," Monroe says, smirking.

"I can take a little more." I stand beside the empty chaise next to Daisy. "Do you mind if I join you?"

"Of course not," Daisy says, rubbing her belly.

I sit. "Actually, this will be a great place to have a wedding."

Monroe grunts while shaking her hands excitedly. "That's exactly what I just said."

Daisy stops rubbing her belly. "I don't know." She looks out over the lay of the land. "Maggie came to live here for a while, and she didn't like at all. I imagine having her wedding in Denver is difficult in itself."

Monroe rolls her eyes as she sighs wearily. She flips on her side so that the front of her body faces Daisy. "Listen, you're a sweet lady—thoughtful and all—but nobody on this planet knows Maggie the way I do. Listen to me; she would love to have her wedding here." She rests her back on the chair again and gets comfortable. "It's Jack's house, and she loves her some Jack."

I hold back a chuckle. In addition to being attractive, Monroe is quite witty.

Daisy sighs. "Perhaps you're right."

"I am right." Monroe takes a sip of wine.

I raise my hand. "Hey, if you need a third aye, then you got mine."

Monroe looks around Daisy and at me. "See… you're not so much of a scoundrel as Maggie made you out to be."

I blink hard. I feel as if she just smacked me in the face with a ton of bricks.

"You can't say that, Monroe," Daisy says, chastising her.

"I didn't mean anything by it. That was a compliment."

Daisy is still reading my expression. She's the kind of person who sees everything, a lot like her husband.

I hold up a hand. "It was no problem."

Monroe's mouth falls open. "Oh shit, did I offend you?"

I twist my mouth. "No…"

"Yes, I did! I'm trying to be more sensitive and shit. Vince's sisters make it hard, but you, Tango, you give me no reason to shoot off my mouth and say whatever the fuck I want."

Daisy and I are speechless. The best thing for us at the moment is to just let the subject of me being a "scoundrel" fade.

"So… are we on with this or not?" Monroe asks Daisy.

Daisy shrugs. "Why not? We're on."

Monroe pumps her fist victoriously. "Yes."

The next topic of conversation is about how Daisy and Jack met. Monroe initiated the subject, but I'm just as interested in hearing how a man lands a woman like Mrs. Lord.

"It just happened between us," Daisy says nonchalantly.

"But you were walking down the aisle in less than a month."

"It was three months."

"What's the difference?"

Daisy studies Monroe like she's trying to get a read on her. "Not much if you think about it. Belmont and I really didn't know each other very well, even if it felt as if we had known each other all our lives."

Monroe grunts cynically. "At first, I didn't think the two of you would last for more than a minute, but then I thought about it. Jack's never been the kind of guy to spread his seed all over the place. I don't know one girl who could claim she fucked him. And let me tell you, I tried, and on many occasions."

Daisy's eyebrows ruffle. "I thought you were about to say something complimentary?"

"Well, yeah…" She aims her finger at Daisy. "You're the one Jack chose, and you didn't even have to stand in line. But I still want to know everything about him."

"Like what?" Daisy's still frowning.

"Like, does he fart in bed?"

Daisy snickers. "All the time."

"I bet it smells like a bed of roses."

"No. It smells like a stinking fart."

I laugh.

Monroe shifts to curl up on her side. " Okay, so does he, like, go to the toilet in general. I always thought he was a god or something. You know they don't shit."

I toss my head back and laugh louder.

I think Daisy says, "Of course Belmont has bowel movements."

"Why would you think Jack doesn't shit?" I ask. I'm extremely curious to know.

"Because unlike the rest of the entire male population, including his backstabbing brother, Charlie, Jack Lord is perfect."

Daisy shakes her head as if that's the dumbest thing she's ever heard. "Believe me, my husband is not a god."

I play along. "Yeah... you're going to also have to convince me that he's not at least a demigod."

Monroe shoots her finger at me. "Right. So let's hear it, Daisy. Let's hear it."

Daisy chuckles as she rubs her belly again. She does that a lot. "Belmont has stinky feet because he wears the same pair of socks over and over. I have to darn near force him to take off his over-worn, offensive smelling socks and throw them in the hamper."

Monroe shakes her head. "You got to do better than that.".

"Okay, well... he has horrible morning breath —oh..." Daisy says abruptly.

"What?" Monroe says as if she's disappointed Daisy stopped.

"He had a decayed tooth in the back. That's what caused the bad breath. Since then, it's been a lot better. Plus, he's... well, *we're* flossing more."

Monroe groans in disappointment. "Shit. That

was going to do it. Halitosis is an intrinsically human condition."

"Well, I've never had it, so what does that make me?" I ask.

"Don't fish, Tango. You're hot," Monroe says.

We all laugh. But as soon as the laughter dies, the silence prevails. I wonder if they feel what I feel. Sure, we're having fun, but I feel guilty about it because Vince is still missing.

"So do you think they found Vince yet?" Monroe asks, her eyes shifting between Daisy and me.

"I haven't heard anything from Jack yet," I say.

"Me, either," Daisy says. "But he'll call me, and when he does, I'll let you both know something."

"Yeah, but it's just strange, don't you think?" Monroe says.

"It's all strange," I say.

"Yeah, but why is Jack out looking for him like he's FBI or something?"

I turn to gauge Daisy's reaction for an answer. She's smiling like she knows something, but she's not saying, and not even poking her on the ass with a hot prod could make her talk.

"Excuse me, ma'am."

We all turn to find a young guy in a black jacket that resembles the one the chef was wearing.

"It's time for dinner. And you also have another guest inside?"

My heart does a jig. I know who it is.

"Is her name Carter?" Daisy asks.

"Yes, ma'am."

Monroe winks at me, and I shake my head to play down my excitement. She's here, and suddenly, I don't know what the hell to do because being around Carter brings out the "scoundrel" in me.

CHAPTER ELEVEN

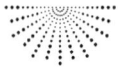

MAGGIE CONROY

*O*ur plane landed in Houston. Anxiety is crawling through my insides like a million tiny ants. Jack has already deplaned. He managed to have Peter Oslo's airplane diverted. I don't know how he did it, but I'm to remain in his jet until he gets back.

I check my watch. Jack left to face off with Peter thirteen minutes ago. I'm sure getting him to divulge Gabrielle's whereabouts won't be easy. If the father is afraid of Jack, he sure as hell wouldn't steer him toward his precious daughter. By the look on Jack's face when he left, he was prepared to extract information from Peter by any means necessary.

"Would you like another latte?" the flight attendant asks.

I'm too nervous to speak, so I can only shake my head.

"Okay, just let me know if you need anything," she says.

Still my jaw won't move, so I nod stiffly.

The minutes pass slowly. I decide to stare at the exit until it opens, hoping that will keep me calm. Suddenly, the door shifts, and the two flight attendants come out from the back and open the doors. I rise to my feet as they lower the ramp.

Plunk, plunk, plunk.

Jack strides into the cabin, carrying the outside air on him.

"What happened?" I ask eagerly.

"One second." Jack sweeps past me and goes into the cockpit.

I hug myself as I wait nervously.

Suddenly, he comes out and flops down in the seat he abandoned. "Buckle up, Maggie. We're going back to New York."

I'm still eager to know more. "But what did Oslo say?"

Jack looks up at me, waiting for me to take my seat.

I sit and buckle up. When I'm secure in my seat my expression begs for an answer from Jack.

"I'm a hundred percent sure he has nothing to do with Vince's disappearance. But I'm certain, as you suspected, his daughter hired Randall to kidnap Vince."

I'm waiting for the part where he says we're closer to finding Vince, but Jack rests his head on the seat as if he's done talking.

"That's it?"

"No, Maggie."

I take a deep breath as a way to rectify my frustration. "Then what?"

Jack turns calmly to face me. "I had Peter call his daughter. Gray tracked the call. She's in the Hamptons, and now that we're tapped into her cell phone, we're tracking her."

"Aren't you afraid Peter is going to tip her off?"

"No."

"Why not?"

Jack gives me that look—the one that I hate. He's not telling me more than he already has.

"Well, can you answer this?"

"Answer what?"

"Are we closer to finding Vince?"

"Yes, we are."

I sit back in my seat, finally at ease and in control. "And he's alive for sure?"

"I can't answer that, but as I said, I believe Gabrielle paid to have Vince kidnapped because he's marrying you. However…" Jack smashes his lips together as he frowns.

The composure I summoned abandons me and I'm about to jump out of my seat again. "However what?"

"I remember Vince was in a relationship with Cindy O'lay."

"Yes," I say impatiently.

"According to Peter, Cindy and Gabrielle are hosting a fashion event together in the Hamptons. He said that they're close friends."

I feel my entire face collapse into a frown as I recall the first time I saw Vince with Cindy O'lay. We were in Iberia at Madam Beauchamp's estate for Charlie and Angel's engagement party. Vince and Cindy O'lay were playing in the pond. My heart nearly shattered into a million pieces later that night when they stopped in front of our table, standing arm and arm. Then, when he finally broke off their relationship to resume ours, Cindy threatened to kill herself. That wasn't even a month ago. And now she's planning a fashion event with Vince's ex-fiancée?

"But I don't understand. Who ordered Douglas Randall to kidnap Vince?"

"Gabrielle did."

"Is that what Peter told you?"

"No."

"Then how do you know?"

Jack blows a sharp breath out of his nose. "Maggie."

"What?" I snap, and then calm myself. I'm pretty sure I'm like a gnat that won't get away from his ear. "I just want this to make sense, Jack."

He studies my tormented expression for a moment, then his eyes soften. "I'm only going with my gut at this time, but I believe that Gabrielle and Cindy O'lay planned Vince's kidnapping together. Gabrielle used her father's resources to do it. Gray checked. The two women have definitely been in the Hamptons this weekend. They've attended three events. However, Vince has not been spotted."

"Do you think Vince is in the Hamptons?"

"That's my educated guess."

I'm facing the brick-wall expression again. Jack is done answering questions. Regardless, he's given me enough information to appease me for the time being, so I sit back in my seat and shake my leg anxiously.

I study Jack. His eyes are closed as if he's meditating. I know how much he hates to be away from Daisy, especially while she's pregnant.

"Jack?" I say quietly.

"Yes, Maggie." I can tell that he's forcing himself to speak calmly.

"Do you miss Daisy?"

"Very much so."

"You should call her and let her know you're fine."

"I will."

After a moment of watching him, I sit back in my seat.

"Get some sleep. When we arrive in Southampton, we're going to have a long night," he says.

I sigh appreciatively. "Thank you."

Jack crushes his lips into a tight smile. "You don't have to thank me. I'll do anything for you. You know that."

I'm so filled with gratitude that my eyes water. "I know."

"Now get some sleep, Magnolia." He opens his eyes to wink at me.

I chuckle. "Okay."

I snuggle my back against the seat and close my eyes. Sleeping is the last thing my brain wants to do. Instead, I reminisce about Hawaii. I force my memory to wrap me in feelings of exhilaration, love, and pure happiness Vince and I generated during that trip. Before I know it, my head and eyelids are heavy. I'm indulging in the memory of sitting on the sand of the private beach that belonged to the house Vince rented in Kauai. Vince's arm is around me, and I'm cuddled up against his chest. As I watched the sun set, I felt love unending, and I still feel it as I drift off into a much-needed sleep.

CHAPTER TWELVE

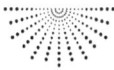

ROBERT TANGO

"Oh, so you're also an architect?" Monroe asks Carter.

"Um-hum," Carter says as she chews.

"Is that how you met?" she asks.

Cater and I glance at each other.

"I assume you two have always been acquainted, but at some point you must've reconnected."

Carter stabs one of the seared scallops on her plate. "And why do you say that?"

Monroe smirks as if she's impressed Carter finally responded. "First, I heard Tango and Vince have been bros even before they had acne and teenage-boy body odor, which means you had to have met him at least once before you…" She

155

shrugs her eyebrows suggestively. "And second, Tango has no interest in me whatsoever, so that means he's very much into you."

The fact that she's right on both accounts leaves me at a loss for words.

Carter grunts inquisitively. "Are you interested in him?"

Monroe shrugs. "If he keeps it up, I will be."

"Keeps what up?" Carter asks.

"Whatever he's doing to change himself." Monroe looks at me and wiggles her finger. "You're not the same guy I met last year."

I still don't know what to say.

"The trick is to keep evolving, which should be the same goal for each of us," Daisy says. I'm sure she senses how uncomfortable I am with this conversation.

"Oh gosh, Daisy," Monroe says. "You'd make a kick-ass politician. Sorry, Tango, didn't mean to make you feel uncomfortable…"

"It's Robert," Carter says.

Monroe flinches. "Excuse me?"

Carter looks her dead in the eyes. "You keep calling him Tango, but his name is Robert."

Monroe glares at her, but Carter continues chewing as if she's unruffled by the daggers

Monroe's eyes are lobbing at her. Suddenly, Monroe sniffs cynically. "Tango? May I call you Tango?"

I really don't want to be in the middle of these chicks. I've never seen Carter this contentious—it's not like her. Grace gave Carter hell for the brief time she worked for me, and she never squared off with Grace like this; and Grace actually gave her a reason to. Something's going on with Carter, and I wonder what it is.

"All you beautiful ladies can call me whatever you want, and I'll answer to it." I paste on a smile, hoping my response was good enough to dissolve the tension in the room.

Carter puts down her fork. "Okay…" She sighs. "I'm going to excuse myself now. Thank you for the dinner and hospitality, Daisy."

Daisy frowns. "You're welcome," she says quietly then scoots back her chair. "How about I come with you to make sure your room is comfortable?"

Carter stands. "Thank you so much, but I'm fine."

Daisy widens her eyes at Monroe as she stands. "No, really, I would love to." She smiles warmly at Carter.

Carter studies Daisy's expression then nods.

As soon as they leave, I turn to Monroe. "Why are you that way?" I ask.

She frowns as if she has no idea what I'm talking about. "What way?"

"You're crass as hell."

She's about to say something, but then she stops. Monroe shifts abruptly to fold her arms on the table, then she uses one arm as a kickstand and presses her mouth against her knuckles as she gazes off thoughtfully. "Have I been a rude bitch?"

"I don't know about the bitch, but you've definitely been rude," I say, figuring this is no time to sugarcoat her behavior.

She looks at me with one eye narrowed then flings her hands out as if she's giving up. "I think I'm going full-on bitch because Maggie left Mo&Ma to marry Vince. You know... I just never believed she would choose being happy homemaker over me."

I snort. "So that's why you're in everyone's ass over this wedding?"

Her frown intensifies. "What do you mean?"

"You're overcompensating."

She grunts thoughtfully. "I guess so. At least that's half of it. I love Maggie, and the bitches of

Vinceville were purposely trying to give her a wedding that's akin to a toothless meth head."

I laugh. "Where do you get this shit?"

Monroe looks utterly confused. "What shit?"

I shake my head. "Forget it."

"Anyway, yes! Yes! Yes!" she shouts to the top of her lungs. "I'm overcompensating. It's just that Maggie… she's always had a better life than I had. Don't get me wrong—I love her to death but, but, damn, I deserve my Prince Charming and happily ever after and shit like that too." She blows a hard sigh. "At least once in my life, damn it."

I blink at Monroe. I don't know what this strange feeling is soaring through me. Maybe the fact that I can relate to everything she just said makes me want to put way more distance between who I'm trying to become and who I used to be.

"Well, you better do something about your envy now, or you'll end up fucking up so badly that Maggie may never forgive you for it."

"You mean do something like fuck Vince?"

I sniff bitterly. "You know about Maggie and me, don't you?"

She smirks. "Every pleasurable detail."

"She liked it?" I say, surprised.

"I'm sure knowing how to fuck is the least of

your problems, Tango," she says in a frank tone. "But if I tell you something, can we keep it just between you and me?"

I take a moment to decide whether or not I want to know whatever sin Monroe is about to confess. She better not have fucked Vince, especially after all the shit he gave me for doing the same with Maggie. The thought of him being hypocritical pisses me off.

I squeeze my lips into a tight frown. "Sure. What is it?"

Monroe smirks as she reads my expression. "It's not that, Tango."

"Not what?"

"The reason why you're putting on that attitude. You see, I tried to fuck Vince, but he wasn't having any part of it. I went over to their house to see Maggie. She wasn't there. He had been swimming, and he was wearing a pair of nut-hugging trunks. I can't deny the guy is hot. I figured there was no time better than now to try to have a piece of Maggie's tasty little pie. I grabbed his cock, and he twisted my fucking arm."

"He did?" That doesn't sound like Vince to be violent like that.

She waves a hand nonchalantly. "He didn't hold

it for long. It was just his initial reaction to me grab-bing his dick. I regretted it as soon as I did it. What the fuck was I thinking?"

I bob my head, recognizing the familiarity between us. "Been there. Except I went through with it."

"Well, it takes two to tango." She winks. "Plus, I know Maggie better than she knows herself. She'll never admit this but she only fucked you just to get back at Vince for firing the first shot."

It takes me a moment to get what she's talking about. "Oh, Emily."

Monroe shoots her finger at me. "Bingo." She shakes her head. "Vince shattered her. It looked like she got over it rather quickly but she didn't. Did she tell you I tried to fuck her after that happened?"

I'm taken aback. Monroe is full of surprises. "Are you a lesbian?"

She squishes one side of her face to think about it. "Mm… I'm what you call fucked up."

"Then you're not gay?"

"I've eaten crack."

Picturing Monroe going down on Maggie turns me on. Then I see her sucking on Carter's soft and tasty clit, and my dick wants to explode. I blink, trying to get ahold of myself.

Monroe is watching me with a wicked smirk. "I wouldn't dare take advantage of you in this state, Robert Tango, especially since you'll only regret it in the morning." Monroe glances over her shoulder. "I guess I should apologize to Carter in the morning. You know she thinks we're fucking, right?"

I frown, taken aback. "No way."

"Yes way. Does she know about your infamous reputation?"

I press my lips together as I nod slowly. "Yep. It followed me to RT Creative."

"Then that's it. She doesn't trust you. She thinks you're the type of guy who'd fuck a frog if you thought it was sexy enough."

I frown perplexed. "Fuck a frog?" *Could you do that?*

One of the servers comes out of the kitchen. "Will it be just the two of you for dessert?"

Monroe and I look at each other.

"Sure." She shrugs. "And a bottle of wine?" she asks me.

"As long as we're sharing it."

Daisy returns to eat dessert with us. She tells us that Carter is fine—she excused herself because she was tired. I'm surprised Monroe doesn't refute the claim. Instead, Monroe and I down an excellent bottle of wine while she expels stories about her celebrity clients and the shit she's had to do for them to save their reputation.

Monroe picks up the bottle and pours the last two glasses of wine. "Shit, I've been talking too much." She frowns curiously. "Daisy, what is this elixir?"

Daisy squints at the bottle Monroe just slammed on the table. "It's *Mes Fleurs Bordeaux*, my father's brand."

"Holy hell sexy apothecary, thou expensive wine is quick." She massages her temples. "So quick."

I can feel the room spinning too. I rest my head back on the chair.

"The great Jacques Blanchard is your dad, right?" Monroe asks.

Daisy cracks a smile. "Yes indeed."

"So we do have something in common," Monroe says excitedly. "We're both children of famous people!"

"Didn't you write a memoir about Clara Richardson?" I ask.

Monroe lifts a finger. "Number-one New York Times best seller for three weeks in a row."

"Congratulations," Daisy says.

Monroe smiles. "Thanks. Oh, and I know your mother too. She's a tough cookie."

"Ah… Heloise, yes."

"You're nothing like her."

"Nope."

Monroe grunts contemplatively. This is the second time she's let a subject drop even though it's clear she wants to pry. The conversation somehow turns to all of us taking a trip to Bordeaux for the Chateaux Mes Fleurs wine festival. Then we end the night playing a game Monroe starts called "let's find a bad bone in Daisy's body." Before Monroe and I figure out we're too drunk to sit at the table any longer, we learn Daisy's not much of a curser or a drinker and has never done hard drugs. However, she does admit that the first time she was pregnant, she thought she was being punished for getting caught up in a whirlwind affair with Jack.

"He asked me to marry him one week after we met, and I said yes!"

"Yeah, that was quicker than your wine," Monroe says.

"Yes…" Daisy sighs. "What Belmont and I have is rare." She rubs her belly. "But if my daughter does what I did, I would lock her in her room until she comes to her senses." She chuckles. "And so would Belmont."

"Why don't you call him Jack?" Monroe asks.

"Because calling him Belmont makes me always remember our Martha's Vineyard love story."

It's quiet. I wonder if Carter and I have a San Francisco love story. I felt something for her that I never felt for any woman. I still feel it.

"Goddamn it, I want my own love story," Monroe says.

Daisy smiles. "Just keep growing up, and you'll have one."

Monroe studies her with a smile

After that, we call it a night and retire to our rooms. I collapse on top of my bed and stare at the ceiling.

"Stay away from her, Robert," I mutter.

Humph. Monroe said that Carter suspects something is going on between us. Does that mean she's jealous? I roll off the bed and scramble to the door. There's nothing wrong with going to check on her. I squeeze the knob and stop. First I have to find her. It shouldn't be hard. I know where Monroe and

Daisy are sleeping. I'll check every other room but theirs.

I pull open the door and rush into the hallway in time to catch Carter shuffling toward the stairwell.

"Carter?" I say loudly, thrilled and surprised to see her.

She stops in her tracks then slowly turns to face me.

I want to focus on her body in the thin cotton dress. I'm guessing it's what she wears to bed.

Her eyes are wide. "Oh, hi, Robert. I was just, um…"

Carter wears a distinct perfume. Ever since I smelled it on her, I started recognizing the scent whenever I'm near a woman who has it on. The floral fragrance surrounds me.

"Were you just at my door?" I ask.

"Um, no," she says.

She *was* at my door. I grin. "Because if you were, you can come on in."

Carter glances over her shoulder like she wants to escape. "Are you alone?"

So Monroe was right. "I don't want to be alone." I wait with bated breath for Carter's reply. I would understand if she turns me down. I'm pretty sure she can tell that I want to take that dress off her, spread her across my bed, and taste her wetness.

"Um, sure," she says.

I blink, surprised. "Really?"

"Unless…"

"No," I say in a rush. "Please come in."

Carter nods and moves in my direction. I finally remember how tipsy I am—and that's another reason why my head is spinning. My desire is running high. I can't ever remember wanting a woman this bad before.

Suddenly, there's giggling coming up the stairs, and before Carter can make it to my door, two women step up into the hallway.

"I'm guessing that one's off-limits," a beautiful brunette says.

The other one is blond, and she's also pretty. When I look closely, I can barely tell she's pregnant. I think I recognize them from Maggie's birthday party, but I'm not sure. When I turn back to Carter, she's observing me.

"Good night, Robert," she says sternly and gusts past the two women.

Looking confused, the women watch her then turn their expressions on me.

"Aren't you Robert Tango?" the brunette asks. She reminds me of that model, Alessandra Ambrosio

"Yep," I say, still wanting to run after Carter.

"Do you remember me?"

I look away from the abandoned stairwell to squint at her face. "Sort of. I think I met you at Maggie's birthday party two years ago."

"Um-hmm," she croons seductively. "You hit on me at both of Maggie's parties."

I shake my head at my past behavior. "I'm sure I did."

She smirks like she's ready to take Carter's place in my bed. "The first time, you were drunk, and the second time, I guessed it was coke?"

It sounds like she's asking me what I was high on. "The hell if I know." I did just about everything —coke, weed, speed, prescription drugs, and ecstasy. However, I drew the line at heroin and crack. I needed to do drugs I knew I could come back from.

She struts in my direction. I try not to pay attention to her ultra-tight jeans and perky tits. "Anyway, I'm Hannah."

We shake hands.

The pregnant one walks over to shake my hand too. "And I'm Cleo."

Finally, the names ring a bell. "Now I remember you. You're the married one."

Cleo smiles. "That would be me."

Hannah bats her eyelashes at me. "So Tango, you seem to be in your right mind tonight. If you need a bed-buddy, I can just park with you," Hannah says.

I narrow my eyes at her thighs and puffy tits. I get a sick feeling in the pit of my stomach, but it passes quickly. What I have now that I didn't have the drunken night that I hit on her is clarity. "I really appreciate the offer, sweetie, but I'm going to have to pass."

She smirks, laying it on thick. "Really, why?"

I consider telling the truth but decide it's not best in this case. "I'm very tired," I say.

Hannah grunts thoughtfully and glances curiously at the stairwell Carter just ran down. "Well, just to let you know, it's a standing offer." She winks at me and continues strolling up the hallway.

Cleo rolls her eyes as she sighs. "Ignore her. She's horny."

I chuckle uncomfortably. There was a time when

I would've loved to do something about Hannah's horny condition. But all I can think of is how Carter will feel about it. I don't want to mess things up with her. So I wave a hand and say a final good night to Cleo and Hannah and go back in my room.

I stand by the closed door, looking out the dark window, wondering why Carter walked away as if I'd done something to her. The more I start paying attention to women, the harder they are to decipher. I close the curtains and climb in bed. A large part of me wants to go downstairs to find Carter. The smaller, and more sensible, part of me sighs in relief for just dodging a bullet. I'm not ready to make love to Carter. Here's a question for Dr. Mahoney, my therapist—how long will it take for me to trust myself? I'm just not sure that I've put enough distance between the old me and the new me I hope I'm becoming.

CHAPTER THIRTEEN

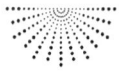

MAGGIE CONROY

"**S**leep well, my love," I hear Jack whispering. "I love you too." He moans softly. "Bye."

I turn to face Jack. "Was that Daisy?" I say tiredly.

"You're awake? Good. We're about to land soon, so if you have to go to the lavatory, now's the time."

I check my watch. I've been asleep for three hours. "Okay." I unbuckle my seat belt and stand. "So how's Daisy doing?" I yawn and stretch.

Jack looks up at me with a gloomy expression. I can tell he misses her a lot. "She's doing good. Oh, and she wanted me to let you know that they've changed the venue of your wedding."

My eyes expand. "They did?"

"Apparently, Monroe has been fighting the rounds with Vince's sisters and beating them up badly."

"Yikes." I don't know how I feel about that. Monroe can be quite a lot to take.

"Don't worry. Daisy has kept her in line, although Monroe had a great idea."

"Really? What is it?"

Jack flashes his signature lopsided smile. "It's a surprise. It's a good one, though. I can vouch for that."

I narrow an eye. "And you're not going to tell me."

"Daisy made me promise."

I want to beg him to give me the answer, but leaving the new wedding venue a secret gives Vince and me something to look forward to.

I take a few more steps toward the lavatory then turn to Jack. "Do you think this is going to end well?"

"You've already asked me that," he says.

"I know but I need to hear the answer again."

He stares into my eyes. "You want the truth?"

I shake my head. "Only if you're optimistic."

"I'm optimistic," he says.

That's it. I'm all good. I gait toward the bathroom feeling about than I did a second ago.

WHEN THE PLANE LANDS, JACK AND I EXIT. IT'S three o'clock in the morning and still dark out. I drive the burgundy BMW, and Jack rides in the passenger seat. The address I'm driving to has been plugged into the Navigator on the dashboard, and the voice-activated Navigator is telling me where to make turns. Jack has a headset on, and I'm sure he's talking to Gray because he's getting updates on where Cindy and Gabrielle have gone in the last ten hours or so. Apparently, they never leave Gabrielle's mansion at the same time.

I'm so involved with trying to piece together Jack's conversation with Gray that I nearly miss my turn. I whip a quick right. The car skids, and Jack holds on to the dashboard.

"Maggie, pay attention to what you're doing," Jack scolds me.

"I am. I just want to know what Gray is saying, that's all."

To my surprise, Jack presses a button on the console. "Repeat that."

Gray hesitates. "Well, per your agreement with Oslo, there's no calling the authorities, no one dies and the girls are unharmed."

"Right, which means I'll use KZR-80 pellets, it'll knock them out cold. I'll try to go in quietly, recover Vince and get the hell out without confronting the opposition," Jack says.

Suddenly, I'm livid. "Wait. You knew where they were keeping Vince ever since you spoke to Peter Oslo?"

"No, I didn't."

"Sounds like it."

The Navigator tells me to take a left at the next light.

Jack sighs exasperatedly. "Maggie, you know I would never withhold that kind of information from you. Gray has been working overtime keeping tabs on Gabrielle and Cindy. He watched their movement patterns. We're not positive they're holding Vince at the Southampton estate, but the chances are that it's where he is. For the past two days, at least one of them has remained in the house at all times."

"I already pieced that together," I say.

"There's a brunch at ten a.m. Both O'lay and Oslo have plans to attend," Gray says.

Jack pins his gaze to the screen on the dashboard. "Can you confirm that the two suspects are planning on being there at the same time?"

"It's definite," Gray says.

"Good. Send me the blueprint."

The voice tells me to make a right turn. I do it, and I'm now driving down a street where the trees create a canopy across the road. The multimillion-dollar estates lining the street aren't visible, but their large iron and wooden gates are.

"Within vicinity of destination," the robot voice says.

"Slow to one mile per hour," Jack says.

I do as I'm told.

"See the white gates to your left?"

My eyes locate the gate. "Yes."

"They're opening. In this order—turn off the headlights, make a left in that drive, and stop when the voice tells you to."

I nod nervously and execute Jack's instructions.

"Stop here," the voice projecting through the speakers says.

I'm only able to see a bunch of trees. We're at the start of a long driveway.

"Is this the house?" I ask.

"The Oslo estate is up the road."

I squint at the tall trees. There are so many of them that it makes the early morning extra dark.

"Who does this house belong to?" I ask.

"It's unoccupied at the moment," Jack says.

I get it now. This is where we stay to keep out of sight. "So are we going to wait here until ten?"

"No." Jack reaches under his seat for his bag and takes out a gun.

I cringe at the deadly weapon. The gun looks even more lethal as he screws on a silencer. My heart is beating a mile a minute. "What do you need that for?"

Jack puts on a black ski mask. "I'm not going to shoot bullets."

I want to gasp at how menacing he looks but instead I close my eyes and snap my fingers, recalling what he said a few minutes ago. "You're going to use KZR-80 pellets.

"Good memory. I'll be back. Stay put," he says.

"You're going to Oslo's way before 10:00 a.m.?"

Jack opens the door. "Just stay put, and don't open the door for anyone."

"But——"

He shuts the door then moves into the trees, blending into the darkness.

I face forward and fill my lungs. When I exhale,

it sounds like a deflating balloon. There's nothing to do at this point but wait, and I've accepted that. I sit very still and count each minute. Thirty minutes feels like an hour, and forty-five minutes feels like three hours. Jack has been gone an awfully long time. The top of the sun is forcing away the darkness.

My eyelids are heavy. I blink just to keep my eyes open. I twist my wrist to look at my watch: 5:47 a.m. Jack has been gone for over two and a half hours. I string together a bunch of curse words and recite them under my breath. I guide my seat back and close my eyes. I might as well try to get some rest since there's nothing for me to do but wait. But what if Vince is nearby? I call up all the energy in my body and visualize myself pushing it out past the trees and across the space that's between us.

"Vince, can you feel me?" I whisper.

VINCE ADAMS

Vince woke up abruptly. "Maggie?" He gasped.

He still couldn't figure out what in the hell had happened to him. After his jog, a car stopped in front of his mother's house. The back window rolled down, and a guy in a suit said he needed to speak to Vincent Adams.

For some reason, he felt compelled to take his phone out of his pocket. "That's me," he said.

He recognized the guy's face, although he couldn't remember from where. Before he knew it, the guy was getting out of the car. His instincts told him to get away, but he stood his ground.

"You should come with me," the guy said.

"Do I know you?" Vince asked.

Suddenly, the guy threw a punch. Vince blocked the blow. The impact was hard. It was clearly meant to hurt him.

"What the hell!" he shouted and tried to clock the guy upside the head with his cell phone. He made light contact, but his cell phone slipped out of his hand. Next, he felt volts of electricity shooting through his body. He thought his insides were exploding. Then, although it went dark, he could still feel the intense shock. The pain became less and less, until there was nothing.

The first time he blinked to consciousness, he was lying on a stretcher. Bright light stabbed him in the eyes. Vince thought he might have been dead. He was not in a rush to face the hereafter, not without first marrying and living his life with Maggie, so he closed his eyes and drifted off again. The next time he opened his eyes, he was in total darkness. He was thirsty, hungry, and alone. He was also shivering cold, but not because the air was cold —something inside him was bringing his temperature down.

"Maggie?" he called. Maybe she could explain what the hell was going on.

"Maggie!" he called louder. His head throbbed.

A door slid open. Light flowed into the room. Vince could make out a female form, tall and thin, standing in the entrance. He recognized her perfume. She said something, and two men walked in. He tried to yell for Maggie again, but the cold sensation rolled through his body, and he was back to wondering if he was dead or alive.

"You're alive, Vince," Maggie said.

They were lying on a bed of clouds, staring into each other's eyes. Finally, she had said to yes to marrying him, and she meant it. There would be no namby-pamby where their relationship was concerned, he was sealing the deal. Vince wanted to reach out and run his hands through her soft hair. Maggie had the most beautiful eyes and kissable red lips. Of course he was dead, and in heaven because Maggie's an angel.

"But if you are here with me, then you must be dead too," he said.

"We're not dead, my love. I just called for you. Listen for me. Come back to me." She reached out to pet his cheek. "Please."

Vince blinked. His eyes opened, and darkness surrounded him. Physically, he was in the same shape he was in the last time he came to—cold, thirsty, hungry, and alone. But this time, he knew not to call for Maggie because she could not hear him.

He recalled the car that stopped in front of his mother's home. It was a black Cadillac. Vince recognized the guy who got out of the back seat. He used to see him going in and coming out of Peter Oslo's office sometimes. The man's name still eluded Vince, but he always questioned whether the man was legit or not. He always looked ready to fight.

Vince checked his pockets. "Shit," he muttered, remembering that he lost his phone. He was shivering so badly that his teeth wanted to chatter. That's when he noticed an IV in his arm. Someone must've been shooting him up with a drug to keep him weak and unconscious. He carefully took the needle out of his arm to keep the drug from flowing through his bloodstream.

Just that one act alone made him very tired. Vince gritted his teeth and remained very still. There were noises nearby. He closed his eyes to help concentrate on the voices.

"I'll hear if he wakes up," a man said.

"We only have one more day here, then I want him transported to the island."

"Um, are you sure this is what Mr. Oslo wants?" He sounded doubtful.

"Don't you ever fucking question my father's orders, Doctor. Yes, that's what my father wants."

Now Vince recognized the woman's voice. It was Gabrielle Oslo. Nobody said "father" the way she said it. When they were engaged, she said that word at least a hundred times a day.

Vince wanted to shout to release all his frustration and anger. Fucking Gabrielle kidnapped him! He wasn't surprised. Taking what she wanted was right up her alley. He would've awakened with a gasp or a wail this time, but thanks to the angel in his dream, he woke up more alert.

He didn't know why, but he could feel Maggie's presence. Now that he was awake, all he had to do was get through the shivers. Once he was more stable, he would have more strength. Vince fought exhaustion until it was easier to keep his eyes open. He imagined being swaddled in Maggie's warm softness. Slowly, the thirst became less intense, and the shivering came to a halt. Breathing got easier. He needed a plan to get out of the mess he was in, or he would find himself back at square one.

He felt as though he heard the voices speaking hours ago, but he remembered Gabrielle saying that she wanted to move him to an island. What the hell was she planning? He was sure Gabrielle had lost her fucking mind. *I can't go to an island,* he thought. He had to marry Maggie, and the sooner, the better. Vince knew he would have to fight for his freedom so that he could find his way back to Maggie.

With each passing moment, Vince considered whether or not now was the time. He was afraid to fail, but he decided there was no time better than the present to act.

The fake groan came deep from within him. Once he'd started, there was no turning back. A lock clicked, and the door slid open. Was he being kept in a shack? The figure of a man walked toward him, slowing, checking out the scene. The trick was to not make a lot of noise so that he could still appear weakened by whatever they were pumping into his bloodstream. Vince called upon all of the strength in his body. Aided by the streak of bright light coming from outside the room, Vince saw that the man had a syringe in one hand. Right before the man pushed the needle into the IV bag, Vince used all his strength to shove the heel of his palm against the guy's nose. The man gasped but didn't drop the needle.

Somehow, Vince found the agility and strength to spring off the bed and grab the man from behind as he smashed his hand over the man's mouth. Vince kept his eye on the door as he fought to keep control of the situation and get the needle out of the man's hand. The guy was trying to yell for help, and to Vince's surprise, no one was coming.

The guy made the mistake of trying to stab him in the thigh with the needle, and that was when Vince was able to get it out of the guy's hand and stick him in the chest. Vince released the drug into the man's body, and slowly he stopped struggling against Vince's grip.

He took a few seconds to gather his bearings. Finally, he turned to look at the doorway—the way out. He ripped off the tubes that were taped to his arm, and he was about to make a run for it when he realized he was wearing the same thing he had on the day he was taken. He thought he should at least wear the guy's green sweatshirt. Vince quickly shed his shirt and stripped the shirt off the man he had subdued. He put it on and laid his shirt over the guy. Then Vince realized he wasn't wearing shoes. He pulled off the guy's shoes and put them on. Miraculously, they fit.

Next, Vince moved toward the light and slowly poked his head out the door. The light stung his eyes, so he had to blink until his pupils adjusted. To his left, a chair sat beside a table, with the *New York Times* resting on top. To his right was a flight of stairs. He looked toward the door at the top—that was the way out. Very slowly, Vince proceeded up the stairs. The door at the top was already cracked open. One look told him exactly where he was: Peter Oslo's house in the Hamptons. He'd been there many times with Gabrielle. He was about to open the door farther, but the sound of two men talking stopped him.

"She's a crazy bitch acting on her own," one guy said.

"Peter's paying us, though," the other said.

"She's got access to his cash. I'm telling you— it's not him; it's her."

The first man sighed exasperatedly. "I tried to call him, but I can't reach him."

"This guy down there... I say we dump him and then get the hell out of here."

"Then we won't get paid."

"Fuck getting paid! I also heard that Red Cloud is on the move because of this shit."

"What?" The guy sounded scared out of his mind. "I heard he was dead."

"Well he isn't. And somehow, this guy is tied to him."

"Fuck, fuck, fuck!" the man cursed. "We have to fucking tool up. We can't reach Peter, and Red Cloud is on the move. He's fucking coming here."

"What about this guy?"

"Are you ready to die?"

"No."

"Then let's get the fuck out of here."

"What about Pacey and Clint?"

The one guy paused. "Shit, fuck 'em. They've been up her ass since this shit started. They probably think she's going to give them a piece."

"Let's go, then."

Vince listened as the men stomped off. Something told him to wait for a second. After a brief silence, he heard someone cursing under his breath.

His footsteps got closer. Vince's back hugged the wall. Another physical battle was on the horizon, even though weakness was setting in again. Vince prayed the man would change his mind and walk the other way. The door opened, and Vince was face-to-face with a man twice his size who was wearing a gun holster with a weapon inside.

"Is he okay, Doctor?" the guy asked.

He followed the man's eyes down to the left side of his chest—to a nametag that read Dr. Wallace Connors. What luck! "Yes, he's fine."

The man observed him with furrowed brows. "You've been pulling double duty, doc. There's breakfast in the kitchen."

Vince nodded stiffly, unable to believe he was pulling this off.

"I'll go check on him myself, make sure he's breathing and shit."

Vince wanted to tell him there's no need, but just getting out of the house without raising further suspicion was more important. Again, he nodded. "Okay, then I'll just go to the kitchen and get some breakfast."

Vince walked fast, but not too fast. As soon as the door closed, Vince walked faster. He followed the sunlit hallway to the back door, remembering the route from the last time he was in the house as he passed them.

Suddenly, the bathroom door opened, and Vince stood looking at Gabrielle Oslo, who was blocking his path. He couldn't believe how summery she looked wearing a yellow sundress and a lacy hat. Where the fuck was she going while she was holding him captive?

Her eyes widened with shock. "What are you doing out?"

Vince panicked, knowing there were some really bad and big guys in the house, carrying guns.

"He got out!" Gabrielle shouted.

Vince ran toward her and pushed her out of the way. Gabrielle stumbled backward into the bathroom. He had never put his hands on a woman, but Gabrielle deserved it. Gabrielle continued to scream bloody murder.

Vince was almost to his destination when he heard, "Vince, stop now or else!"

He turned to see Cindy standing down the hall, next to a man who was pointing a gun at him.

Vince put his hands up. A few more steps, and he would've been home free. Gabrielle picked herself up off the floor, screaming about how he hurt her and how he's always hurting her.

"Well, not anymore," Gabrielle said, stalking toward him.

Suddenly, glass shattered, and the guy with the gun fell backward. Cindy screamed. The gunman lay on the floor knocked out cold. The second gunman, the guy who'd told Vince to get breakfast, ran into the hallway from the basement.

"What the hell is going on?" His eyes grew wide as soon as he saw his partner. There was another muffled sound of a gunshot, and the other guy hit the floor.

Cindy screamed again and stutter-stepped as though she wanted to run away but knew it was her mess lying at her feet.

Suddenly, a man in a black ski mask walked in through the door Vince was trying to escape through.

Frozen in place, Gabrielle and Cindy watched him.

"Go, Vincent." His voice sounded distorted.

With adrenaline pumping through his body, Vince bobbed his head wildly then ran toward the door. Each stride was a struggle, but he had all the will in the world to keep moving. Finally, the outside air hit his face. He was free. The farther he got from the main house, the safer he felt. Yet, he was still vulnerable. Vince searched the trees for more gunmen. So far there were none.

When he first met Gabrielle, his instincts warned him to stay away. He would've ended their relationship long before he met Maggie, but by then, Gabrielle was using her father to keep them together. And Peter Oslo was happy to deliver him to her. She was crazy then, and even crazier now.

Vince reached the end of the driveway. He paced along the pavement, still careful to stay out of sight. The gate could've opened at any second, and anyone could've driven through, even Peter Oslo. Vince's adrenaline levels began to subside. His legs shook, and his arms dragged. The extreme cold sensation returned with a vengeance as it surged through him. Suddenly, the environment spun, and his breaths became shallow. *Keep standing. His rescuer will be here soon,* he told himself. But he was losing the battle against consciousness. Vince collapsed to his knees, then his face hit the lukewarm pavement.

MAGGIE CONROY

I feel the car power on without my doing. I open my eyes and rub them, wondering how long I've been asleep. I check my wristwatch. 8:11 a.m. The console flashes and chimes, and I lift my hands off the steering wheel.

"Maggie, back out of the gate and follow the instructions to where I am," Jack's voice says, coming out of the speaker.

The gate behind me slides open.

"Where are you?" I ask, but Jack is no longer on the line. After I back out, the woman's voice tells me to make a left and proceed four hundred feet before turning right. I look ahead. I can see a gate slide open. I'm sure that's my destination. I speed up and cut a sharp right. Jack is alongside the driveway, kneeling next to Vince, who's lying on the ground.

I stop the car, throw the gearshift in park, and jump out. I fall on my knees next to Vince. "Vince?" He's out like a light. I look at Jack. "Is he okay?"

"Help me get him in the car."

Jack curls his arms under Vince's shoulders and lifts him, and I lift Vince's legs. I can't take my eyes off his face. Although he's unconscious, Vince looks as if he hasn't had a lick of sleep in the last two days. Jack does most of the heavy lifting, but we finally get Vince in the car. Jack drives. I sit in the backseat with my love. I put his head on my lap and rub his scalp, hoping at some point he'll wake up.

AN HOUR LATER, WE'RE AT JACK'S SOUTHAMPTON mansion on Meadow Lane. I'm lying next to Vince in a king-sized bed. Dr. Borneo and two nurses have been flown in on a helicopter from New York. They've been tending to Vince ever since we arrived. Right now, they're flushing Vince's system and giving him the nutrients he's been lacking. He hasn't opened his eyes yet, and I haven't stopped worrying even though Dr. Borneo said he'll make a full recovery.

Jack and I had a talk. Since Vince and I will soon be husband and wife, and he doesn't advocate secrets between spouses, he agreed to let me tell Vince everything. But the truth of how he saved him stops with us.

"So I shouldn't tell anyone Vince was kidnapped," I say.

"Use your instincts, Mags. That's all I'm asking.

However, the truth about the part I played, remains a secret to everyone else but Vince."

I nodded, letting him know I'll respect his wishes.

Now, I'm lying on my side facing Vince. I showered while they hooked Vince to monitors and IVs. Jack let me wear one of Daisy's night slips, so I'm finally clean and comfortable. If only Vince would open his eyes. At least the color is coming back to his face. What a handsome man he is. I want to cuddle up next to him, but I promised the doctor that I would keep my distance until he opens his eyes. However, I reach out and take his hand and hold it—this sort of touching has been approved.

CHAPTER FOURTEEN

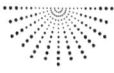

ROBERT TANGO

*I*t's crazy around here and back at the office in San Francisco. My phone has been ringing nonstop. On top of that, I've been trying to get ahold of Jack ever since I was awakened by the morning breakfast bell. Still, he's unreachable. I got dressed, went downstairs, and joined the women at the table.

Now we're halfway through breakfast; Daisy is called away from the table to take an important call. I set my eyes on Carter again—she hasn't looked at me once since I sat down.

"So, Robert, where are you living in San Francisco?" Hannah asks. She's still grinning and batting her eyelashes at me.

I clear my throat as I steal another glance at Carter. She doesn't look away from her plate.

"I'm staying in Jack's place in Russian Hill. Well, right now it's Jack's house; he's agreed to entertain my offer to buy it from him."

"Oh," Hannah says, sounding impressed. "You're a very successful man, aren't you?"

Monroe grunts as though she's heard enough. "Stop, Hannah. You're striking out, and it's torture to watch."

Hannah rolls her eyes. "Oh, be quiet, Monroe. You don't know what you're talking about."

"Tango is not into you." Monroe winks at Carter, who's finally looked up from her plate, and Hannah sees it.

Carter drops her face again, but this time, she does it bashfully. I was a little leery of Monroe at breakfast yesterday, but I'm starting to like her, a lot.

"So what's your name again?" Hannah asks, pointing at Carter.

I feel tightness in my chest. I don't want Hannah giving Carter any shit now that she knows who I'm really into.

Carter flexes her eyes at Hannah for a moment. She sits up straight in her seat. "My name is Carter."

"Oh. And what do you do?"

Carter frowns. "What do you mean by 'what do I do?'"

"Like, for a job—for a living."

"I'm an architect. What do *you* do?"

Hannah flinches, seeming surprised. She's discovered the one thing that made me fall for Carter. She's like a piñata. On the outside, she's a lot of beautiful colors, gorgeous with a delicate form. But just break her open, and she's filled with sweet and delectable surprises. She's tough, able to hold her ground against any bitch.

"I'm a stylist and photographer. So if you ever want to do something about your image, then call me. I'll leave you my card." She smiles patronizingly.

Carter's frown intensifies. "Excuse me, but what do you think needs to be fixed on me?"

"Nothing," Monroe says before Hannah can speak.

Everyone at the table looks at Monroe.

"Everybody can use something," Hannah says.

"Humph." Monroe puts her finger on her lower lip thoughtfully. "I think we have outgrown each other, you know."

Hannah grimaces. I don't think she was expecting Monroe to say that.

"Because, you know… you can't go around telling perfectly beautiful women that they need to fix their fucking image. I fix images for a living, and this one here"—she thumbs over at Carter—"has nothing wrong with hers. So lay off of her, Hannah." Monroe wipes her mouth. "I'm done eating." She pushes her chair back, gets out of her seat and storms away from the table.

I'm about to go after her, but Daisy strolls into the room. Monroe stops because Daisy's smiling widely.

"What's going on?" she asks.

Daisy puts her hands on Monroe's shoulders. "Vince, Maggie and Belmont are coming home."

Monroe expels a sigh of relief and grabs on to Daisy.

I sigh in relief too. It feels as though I'm living in a whole new reality now that Vince has been found.

"So where was he?" Monroe asks.

Daisy looks at her questioningly.

"Hannah and Cleo knows. I told them. Maggie would tell them. We tell each other everything," Monroe says.

Daisy nods, and they both return to their seats at the table. Monroe takes a second to snub Hannah. I don't think what's going on between them has anything to do with Carter or me.

Daisy expounds on how loony-tune Gabrielle and Cindy O'lay both kidnapped Vince just so that he would miss his wedding day.

"But how did Jack and Maggie find him?" I ask.

"Belmont said they asked around the Hamptons," Daisy says.

There's something very incomplete about Daisy's answer, and her pasted-on smile proves she knows it.

"Who did they ask?" Monroe says, taking the words right out of my mouth.

Daisy shakes her head innocently. "I don't know. Belmont didn't give me many details. However, he did say that Vince ended up escaping."

"Oh…" Monroe looks even more confused—just how I feel. She and I look at each other.

"The good news is that Vince is safe and sound. They'll be back tomorrow, so we have a lot of work to do before Saturday," Daisy says.

I have to admit that she's good at keeping the control. I figure I can go along with it for now because all that matters is Vince is safe and sound.

I rub my hands together. "So what can I do to help?"

Daisy flashes her influencing smile. "Happy you asked. I was wondering if you can handle the tent for the reception. We need something grand," she says, gesturing with her hands. "I figure we should have the wedding by the lake and the reception in the garden. I want to bring in more springtime flowers and use them as a backdrop."

"I'm on it."

"Great, and I'll give you my credit card details for payment."

I wave a hand. "No way. This is on me. It's the least I can do for Vince and Maggie."

"Okay, what about me?" Monroe asks.

"You and I are going to work on securing all the bells and whistles for the wedding. You know, doves, flamingos, exotic flowers, my dad's band, streets of gold, a crystal stage, a glowing dance floor and stuff like that." Daisy winks at Monroe.

Monroe chuckles and claps her hands. "I like your style."

"I guess I can help Robert with the tent," Hannah says.

"No, I think that job is best suited for Carter, since she's the other architect. I think your skill set is best suited for helping decorate for the ceremony. We want extravagance. We want the guests to be swept off their feet and taken to an enchanted universe."

Hannah shrugs indifferently. "Okay. Well— that's definitely my forte." She sounds disappointed.

I look at Carter again, and she's still avoiding my glances.

"Oh, and by the way, Carter," Hannah says.

Carter narrows one eye at her. "What?"

"I didn't mean to offend you. You're beautiful, of course, but if you've seen Maggie—well, that's my handiwork. When I look at you, I just see a masterpiece waiting to become. That's all." She sneers at Monroe.

Monroe snorts and rolls her eyes. She obviously doesn't believe Hannah is being genuine. I think she is, though.

"Well, thank you," Carter says.

"You're welcome, and I'm serious."

Before breakfast ends and we all get to our parts, Daisy breaks the news about the venue change to Anne. I don't think she likes having control of planning the ceremony taken completely out of her hands, but at this point, there's nothing she can do about it.

First, I call Zoe and ask if she can find a store in town that sells tents for weddings. She works her magic and gets Carter and me an appointment to speak to a representative at eleven thirty.

I find Carter in the backyard, near the lake, with Daisy and the rest of the ladies. Allie and Anne have joined them. Hannah is giving me the eyes. She's also put on a crop top and a long skirt that hangs on her hips. I don't know what she likes about me. She really doesn't know me that well, and the two times I saw her, I was a mess. Carter, though, now she has a reason to like me. She's only seen the best of me, and we've spent some quality time together.

"Afternoon, ladies," I say.

This time, when I look at Carter, she's already watching me, no—studying me. "Are you ready?" I ask her.

"Ready for what?" She sounds jumpy.

"You're coming with me to the party rental store for the tent."

"Make sure you get a pagoda style tent, large enough for one hundred and fifty guests," Anne says.

I wink at her. "Got it." I was planning on doing that anyway but Anne needed to do some dictating.

She's used to being the one in charge. Daisy and Monroe took that privilege away from her, and despite this one little interference, she's been doing pretty good with relinquishing her power. I set my gaze back on Carter. "So we should go."

"Are you sure you don't need company?" Hannah says. "I've been to a lot of high-end garden parties, so I know exactly how things should look."

"Why don't the two of—"

"That's okay. Carter and I have it covered," I say before Carter can finish throwing me to the wolf. I'm starting to get pissed. "Let's go," I say and start stomping up the lawn.

"See you, Carter," Monroe sings coquettishly. That's the only clue I have that Carter's following me. As soon as I make it to the side of the house, I turn to look behind me. She's not that far away. However, she's close enough that I notice how her yoga pants outline her pussy print. The shit I notice about a woman. I shake my head. What the hell is wrong with me?

I'm all messed up in the head by the time I make it to the car. I open the passenger door for Carter and watch her move closer. I work hard to keep my eyes on her face and not the way her nipples poke the T-shirt she's wearing. The way I feel about Daisy and Monroe proves that I can admire a woman, one I like a lot, without wanting or needing to fuck her.

Carter passes me and gets into the car. "Thank you." She's back to avoiding looking me in the eyes.

My pulse is racing. "Listen, you might not want to have anything to do with me, but it's not up to you to pass me off to other women. So don't do that anymore."

She seems surprised. "Do what?"

"Try to feed me to Hannah."

She folds her arms. "It looked like you wanted to be with her."

"In your head probably, but not in mine."

She opens her mouth to speak then pauses for a moment. Finally, she says, "Okay, sorry. I won't do that anymore."

I nod sternly and carefully close her door. I wanted to slam it, but I didn't want to accidentally crush her fingers or something.

Soon we're on the road. The loudest sound between Carter and me is the smooth purring of the engine. Maybe I should give up on her already. We tried. She doesn't want me, and I think I'm okay with it. There was a time when I wouldn't have accepted the rejection. I had an unrelenting need to be desired by a woman after she rejected me. During one session, Dr. Mahoney led me to the conclusion that my need for approval was the result of seeking love from my mother, who sought to give her love to every man on the planet except me. Then, after, I secretly rejected that notion, but after today, I'm pretty sure it's true.

I sigh the tension out of my shoulders. I'll stop chasing Carter. If she doesn't want me, then so be it. But I don't want Hannah. I'm looking for a different kind of woman in my life—a Daisy or a Maggie, or even another Carter.

"That's not what I was doing," Carter says out of the blue.

I glance at her—shocked that she's speaking.

"I wasn't trying to put you off on Hannah. Actually, I thought the two of you had gotten together after I went to my room."

"Well, you thought wrong."

The air is thick between us. The silence is unwelcome but necessary at this point.

"I'm relieved because she's no good for you," Carter says.

I smirk. "Is that so?"

"She's too superficial. Did you see that outfit she put on? Just for you, of course."

"You seem bothered by it."

She grunts as if she wasn't in the least bit fazed by Hannah's attempt to get my attention.

I snicker. "So how are you getting along in DC, anyway?"

"You asked me that already."

"I did, but I want a different answer this time."

She shrugs indifferently. "It's still just fine. It's different for sure."

"Oh yeah? How?"

"Everything's bigger somehow. Bigger personalities. Bigger streets. Everybody has a big job title. Bigger salaries but friendlier people."

I nod continuously. "You know what? You may not have thought this, but I know exactly what you mean."

"I knew you would get it. Nothing's too complex for you, Robert Tango."

I think back to when I took her to lunch in San Francisco and she tried to trip me up with her esoteric conversation. I realized very quickly that was her way of flirting. I take a quick glance at her to verify that she's flirting with me now. Carter is grinning. I want to pump my fist and say, "yes."

"How's the DC dating scene?" I ask.

She shifts in her seat. "Fine." Once again, she's using a high-pitched voice.

"Have you been on a date?"

"I've been on some dates."

My heart just took a nosedive. "How many is some dates?"

"Just a couple."

"Really? Have you been in DC long enough to find two guys to date?"

"Same guy."

I glance at her again. She's looking straight ahead.

"Then you're seeing someone?"

"No, not really."

"But you went on two dates with one guy?"

She hesitates. "Um, yes."

"Wow…" I scratch my head. The idea of us being together just slipped another mile away. "Well, congratulations."

"For what?"

"Finding someone you like."

I'm so rattled that I almost miss my turn. I jam down on the brakes and put my arm out as Carter shifts back and forward. "Sorry about that," I say as I turn the corner.

She recovers from the jolt. "That's okay. And by

the way, it was just two dates, not a commitment."

I sniff bitterly. "Sort of like what we had." I glance at her.

"No, I never had sex with him," she says defensively.

It falls silent again. Something's happening between us. I think we just reopened that tightly sealed can of worms. "So why did you disappear anyway?" I ask.

"Oh," she says as if that's the last question in the world she wanted me to ask. "Do you want to know the truth?"

"Sure. Yes."

"I went snooping in your office and found those photos."

My eyebrows furrow as I think. It takes a moment, but I remember. "The ones of us in the car together?"

"Yeah... they looked like we were involved, and then we did get involved, so..." She throws her hands up like there's nothing more to say.

"So you decide to make us uninvolved?"

I glance at her and she shrugs indifferently.

I take another quick look at her before pulling in the parking lot of the party-planning place. "I wish you wouldn't have left."

"I wish I wouldn't have left, either."

I pull into a stall then turn to face her. We're trapped in the moment, gazing into each other's eyes.

Suddenly, the phone rings on the console. Grace's name comes up. I contemplate answering her call. I've already spent a ton of time listening to her complain about the bid being submitted without her interior design proposal attached. Just like Gabrielle Oslo, Grace's father nurtured her into a spoiled brat who thinks the world revolves around her.

"Aren't you going to answer it?" Carter asks.

"It's Grace."

"I can see that. You know she's just going to keep calling until you pick up."

"You're right." I sigh and answer the call. "Yes, Grace."

"Just so you know, I submitted my portion with the bid."

"Really? How did you do that?"

"Don't sound so excited, Robert. I know you've never been on my side."

I take a deep breath and run my hands through my hair. "Believe what you will."

"Do you want to know how I was able to submit

after the deadline?"

"Sure. You're going to tell me anyway."

"I know somebody," she answers.

Typical Grace.

Carter nudges me on the shoulder and mouths. "Ask her who?"

I frown, taken aback. "Who?" I ask before I can make sense out of why Carter would want me to ask Grace that.

"Are you in your car?" Grace asks.

"Um, yes."

She snorts cynically. "Is someone with you?"

"What?"

"Carter?" Grace calls.

Carter rolls her eyes like she's been caught. "Hi, Grace." Her tone is deadpan.

"I knew you two would find your way back together at that wedding, but Robert darling, you're fraternizing with the enemy. You see, Metropolis has also put a bid in for the Atlantic Metropolitan Library Project. Haven't you, little Miss Muffet?" Grace says cynically.

"Hey," I chastise. "Play nice."

"You know what? I have nothing else to say to you other than see you Monday bright and early in your office." Grace hangs up.

Carter and I look at each other as if we just experienced a hit and run.

"So what was that anyway?" I ask.

Carter's eyes expand. "I don't know. She's always been wacky."

I shake my head while smirking. "No, not that. You asking me to ask her for the name of her special person."

"Oh…" She grins mischievously.

"Humph…" I narrow my eyes to study her pretty but shrewd face. "Are we at war?"

Carter shrugs. "Maybe. But first let's build Vince and his bride a castle that beats all wedding tents." She holds out her hand for me to shake.

At least I'll be seeing her sooner after the wedding is over than I thought. I know our bid and the one from Metropolis will definitely be among the final bids. Metropolis has an advantage over us, though, because they're already on the East Coast. I will have to station a temporary team in Maryland until I get a full-time office up and functioning there. I want an Atlantic Coast presence. The Atlantic Metropolitan Library Project is going to be RT Creative's first major project in that region, and it's going to put us on the map in no time flat.

I take hold of her hand. "Deal."

We squeeze each other's hands and don't let go. *What if I tugged her closely and kissed her lips?* I ask myself just before our mouths come together. The warmth of her tongue swirls around mine. But we're not going at it all fast and furious. My lips want to take their time with her lips. My tongue wants to taste her deeply. My loins throb for more. My hand slides up her T-shirt and under her bra. I find her tit and squeeze it. My mouth wants to taste her nipple, so it slides down her neck, kissing, biting, and licking.

I step my foot down, and the engine roars. "Shit." I rip my lips off hers.

Carter's eyes are wide and dazed. "We better get inside." She's breathing heavily.

Thank goodness I had the car in park. "Yeah."

She gets out of the car. I'm slightly dizzy as I hop out. We come together on her side. It takes every bit of my willpower not to take her in the backseat.

"Ready?" I say.

She nods.

We trek across the parking lot with the appropriate amount of space between us.

CHAPTER FIFTEEN

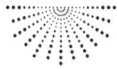

MAGGIE CONROY

*T*he heart monitor beeps out of control. Vince gags, choking. I watch, horrified, as his skin turns blue. I reach out for him, but I can't touch him.

"Maggie?" I hear him say in a calm voice.

I wake with a gasp, facing Vince's bright-green eyes.

His face beams. "Hey, beautiful," he whispers.

Thank God I was dreaming. The color has returned to his skin. There are no tubes or monitors attached to him, and his shirt is off. He looks and smells showered and shaved.

"How long have you been awake?" I ask.

"About two hours. You were tired, babe."

I flip on my back and breathe until the exhaustion passes. "I guess I was. I was just so worried about you."

"Come here." Vince opens his arms to receive me.

I scoot against his warm and hard body, but before we merge, I check his skin for bruises. "No one hurt you?" I ask.

"Not my body anyway." He pulls me against him, and my backside meets his front.

We're so close that it's as if our figures have been glued together. I love being consumed by his heat and feeling his heart beat against my back. Never again do I want to be separated from Vincent Adams. I still have to pinch myself. Never would I have thought when we were in high school that we would end up here together.

"If they didn't hurt your body, then did they hurt your mind?" I ask. I feel his pause.

"It's the week we're getting married, and then this happened. That's what I hate."

"I know," I say with a sigh. "And it was Gabrielle *and* Cindy O'lay." My lips gather tightly.

"I didn't even know they knew each other. When I escaped, I kind of remember running into one or both of them. My memory's foggy, but I think Gabrielle said something about me not getting away from her this time." He grimaces as he thinks. "Then Jack told me to run. I didn't know it was him at first. After I woke up, he told me."

"Everything?" I ask.

"Everything."

I feel so relieved about that. "Yeah... Jack's been surprising through all of this. I don't know who or what he is anymore."

"I always knew he had some clout. He got Peter to sell his stake in my company with no pushback. That guy fights to the bitter end, but he didn't go to war with Jack."

I sigh. "Well, whoever or whatever he is, I'm happy he's my cousin and he loves me. If it wasn't for him, I would've never found you."

"It would've been harder without Jack, but I would've found my way back to you, baby. I was on my way when Jack showed up."

We kiss, and as usual, I turn lightheaded.

"Are you ready to become Mrs. Adams?" he whispers passionately.

I close my eyes and indulgently brush my face against the skin of his chest. "So... ready."

Vince and I lie close for a long time. It's funny... before he was ripped out of my life, I was so yearning to make love to him, but not anymore. I just want his heart, his spirit, and his soul.

"Hey?" he whispers and guides me to turn and face him.

I sniff to stop the tears. My heart was so overwhelmed that I started to cry.

He kisses the wetness on my cheek. "I'm okay."

"I know you are. I just…" I kiss him, and the tears return.

Vince is stimulated by our kiss. He smoothly rolls on top of me, planting himself between my thighs. My knees flow up, and my legs ceremoniously wrap around his lower back. Every body movement, every whirl of our tongues and meshing of our lips is passionate. My soul whimpers and moans because it loves being entwined with his. Vince reaches down to put himself inside me. The pleasure makes me sigh on first thrust. He shifts in and out of me, so slowly and deeply. My insides grasp at his rigidness, tingling with each prod. I wrap my arms him and hold him tightly. I want him so much that I cannot breathe—I cannot live.

"Oh, Vince," I moan.

He releases himself inside me, and I hold him tighter.

"I love you," he says.

"I love you," I say.

Tears trail down my face. I believe we've reached nirvana.

VINCE AND I HAVE OFFICIALLY CAST ASIDE OUR PACT to wait until we're married to make love. We make love many times throughout the day. I only leave him so that the nurses can draw blood. It's also scary to learn that one more dose of what that doctor gave him could've poisoned and killed him. He was lucky to get away when he did.

Jack has already flown back to Denver to be with Daisy. The cook has dinner brought to our room. Dinner is a light, creamy chicken soup souf-flé. After we finish eating, Vince calls his mother and apologizes for leaving so abruptly. I can tell that it kills him to lie to her, but he continues to apolo-gize until she believes him. We cuddle and sleep the night away.

Our flight from Southampton leaves at six in the morning, and we agreed to wait until tomorrow to see the setup for the wedding and reception. However, we are having dinner at Jack's house tonight with our friends, although Vince and

I have been warned not to step foot into the backyard.

As soon as we arrive in Denver, Vince and I go check out of our room at the Ritz-Carlton. One aspect of making Anne happy was agreeing to return to her house for the night. Lexie and Maddie pounce on Vince as soon as we step into the foyer.

"Fancy having you back," Lexie says snottily.

"We were supposed to plan your wedding, not that bitchy harlot," Maddie says.

I'm pretty sure they're referring to Monroe.

Vince sighs tiredly. His arm that's around my waist grips me tighter, and I take it as good sign. "You know, after what you pulled with Emily, I'm not on your side with this one."

Lexie's eyes expand as though he just spit on her. "You promised."

Vince blows a breath that so strong it rattles his lips. "Lexie, not now."

She smashes her hands on her hips. "Then when."

He shakes his head as we look into each other's eyes. "Let's get our stuff to the room. We have a long day."

I nod, and we continue up the stairs. I'm proud of Vince for finally sticking up for himself, and me.

I hear Lexie stomp off and say that she's not going to the wedding.

"Me, neither," Maddie says.

Vince just doesn't seem to give a damn.

My final dress fitting is scheduled at the same time as Vince's suit fitting with his best man and groomsmen. Since we're all going to be drinking champagne, Monroe ordered a chauffeured SUV to take us to my fitting. I'm here with Monroe, Hannah, and Cleo. Being separated from Vince after what we went through is tough, but at least I'll see him at dinner this evening.

"Oh, so really, Cindy O'lay was part of the whole kidnapping scheme?" Hannah asks while sitting in the waiting area.

I cringe while in the dressing room. The saleswoman, Brandy, is zipping the back of my dress, which is a white silky mermaid gown with a sweetheart neckline.

I smile timidly at Brandy. By the look on her face, she's recognized the name. "Can we not talk about that right now?" I say.

"Oh," Hannah says like she just put her shoe in her mouth. "Of course."

"Let's see, let's see, let's see!" Cleo says, clapping her hands.

Brandy steps back to get an eyeful of me. "You're so beautiful," she says earnestly. "Like a goddess."

I smile. "Thank you." I step from behind the curtain and out into the waiting room.

Monroe puts her hand over her mouth and gasps. "Oh my Lord, Maggie, you're a real bride."

I smile squeamishly. "I guess I am."

Cleo is just shaking her head. "I can't believe this is you standing in front of us like this."

I scoff and roll my eyes. "I know, right. Me, Miss *I ain't ever getting married.*"

Hannah is already snapping shots of me. "Stop yapping and pose, damn it," she demands.

I feel divine, so I swish my body this way and that, giving her all kinds of angles. After my one-woman fashion show ends, we sit in the waiting room while Brandy prepares my dress to go, and I drink my second glass of champagne. We reminisce about all the frogs I kissed before Vince, and how I broke up with each of them because of one stupid reason or another.

"There was the farter," Cleo says. "I can imagine Vince not farting."

I sniff a chuckle. "He farts."

Hannah snaps her fingers. "Oh, remember the one who left gobs of toothpaste in her sink?"

"Oh, yes, Mags couldn't have that," Monroe says with a cynical roll of her eyes.

We all laugh.

"Then there was the bad driver," Cleo says.

"The one who couldn't look her in the eyes for more than four seconds," Hannah adds.

I point at each of them. "Never trust a man who can't look you in the eyes."

"But you said Vince couldn't look you in the eyes at first."

I grunt. "True… that's true." My head is spinning. I'm tipsy.

"Then there was the guy who ate with his elbows on the table. Remember that one?" Cleo says.

"The one who stuffed his napkin in his collar," Hannah says.

"Yeah, but… she was right to give that one the boot." Cleo scrunches her nose. "Who does that?"

Monroe sighs. "We can add to the list forever.

But we're not." She lifts her glass. "Cheers to Vince, the one who did not let Maggie get away."

I chuckle and drink to that. I guess I have been finicky in the past. It's funny how quickly the mind recovers from trauma. It's as if Jack's and my expedition to find Vince happened years ago, but our ordeal only ended yesterday. Here I am smiling, happy and excited about taking my vows of forever with the only man I can ever love like this. And it's enough for me to forgive Cindy and Gabrielle for what they've done—at least for now.

FROM THE DRESS SHOP, WE GO TO THE CHERRY Creek Shopping Center so they can buy me something new and something blue. They all chip in to buy me a sapphire-and-diamond ankle bracelet that costs a pretty penny.

On the way back to the house, Monroe assures me that Anne has the something old part handled and Daisy has the borrowed. I also get to hear the play-by-play of Monroe and Daisy's triumph over Lexie and Maddie.

"Now, Allie…" Monroe shakes her finger at me. "She's your ally."

"I know! I was starting to get that before what happened to Vince happened," I say.

It grows eerily quiet. I think they all want to know more but realize that I'd rather not talk about it in detail.

"Well, I'm just glad he's okay," Cleo says.

I smile at her. "Me too."

"Anyway, why haven't you ever told me Daisy is like the coolest?" Monroe asks.

I wiggle my head as though I can't believe she just said that. "I told you that a thousand times."

Monroe tilts her head to think. "Oh, right, you did. But I'm not jealous of her anymore, so…"

I toss my head back and laugh. It feels so good to be this happy again.

Hannah leans over to pat me on the thigh. "Oh, Robert Tango. I like him." Her eyes expand as though she just saw something tasty to eat. "I want him."

"Ugh." Monroe rolls her eyes. "He's not interested in you."

"Not yet. So, Maggie, tell me all about him."

I recall the last two telephone conversations he had with Vince. "Well… he's changed a lot in the last six or seven months, so he's still pretty fragile."

"What do you mean by *fragile*?"

"He realized he was on a road going nowhere, and he wanted to change that. And actually, he has."

"So he's no longer a scoundrel?"

Monroe and I say no at the same time.

"He and I are becoming really good friends," Monroe says while nodding.

Hannah grunts. "Oh, now I get it. *You* want to fuck him."

"No. I don't," Monroe states staunchly.

"Actually, I can see the two of you being friends. You have a lot in common," I say.

Monroe shakes her hands as if to say that's the point. "I know. He actually called his therapist and asked her to recommend someone in LA for me that would be good for someone with his kinds of issues."

"Mommy issues?" Cleo says.

Monroe shoots her finger at her. "Exactly."

"So did the therapist call you?" I ask.

"I have my first appointment next Wednesday." Monroe narrows an eye at me. "By the way, what are you going to do about Mo&Ma?"

I sigh exasperatedly. I really don't want to talk about this at the moment, but there's no better time than the present. I have Cleo and Hannah here to offer guidance. "I don't know, Roe. I really dislike our clients, and I'm tired of forklifting them out of their mountain of shit."

Monroe nods as though she's really considering what I just said. "They are pretty repulsive. I mean Delta?" She shakes her head. "Let's brainstorm, come up with a new way to operate, because we're good together, Mags, and you know it."

Suddenly, I feel this void when thinking of Mo&Ma. "You know, why don't you do something else, Roe?"

"I *am* doing something else. I could be living off my trust fund while fucking pretty boys in exotic destinations."

"True. But you've been running away from your talents ever since we were in the tenth grade. The problem is you want to avoid any parallels with your mother, but remember the time you played Rizzo in *Grease*?"

"I remember that," Hannah says. "You brought the house down."

"You're an actress, Monroe. That movie you made with Charlie about your mother was great and successful. Make another movie and star in it. You have the money and the contacts."

Monroe studies her lap with a grimace. I'm glad

she's doing that. She does that when I strike a nerve.

"I don't know," she finally says with a sigh.

"Well, just think about it. Will you?"

She shrugs. "I will. But you, Hannah, leave Tango alone. He's in love with Vince's cousin."

I frown. "You mean Carter?"

"Yes."

"That's right. They know each other. She worked at the architect firm Vince took over. But now she works in DC."

"So, Monroe... he lives in SF. She lives in DC. And I have an assignment in SF for as long as it takes," Hannah says.

Monroe shakes her head. "You're so selfish, Hannah." She looks at Cleo. "Am I that way?"

"More than Hannah," Cleo says, dishing out a dose of her brutal honesty.

"Then I'm changing." Monroe looks toward the sky. "Hello, shrink, work your magic because I'm tired of being a self-centered, crazy bitch."

"Good luck with that," Hannah says pessimistically.

I snap my fingers. "Okay, let's change the subject. I haven't been a bridezilla, but this is my day, and I want my two besties to quit nipping at each other."

So we move on to whether or not I'm going to change my last name. It's a tough question to answer because I'm the last of the Conroys.

Finally, we make it back for dinner. Charlie and Angelina have arrived, and I'm so happy to see them both. I feel so bad about downplaying such a big event like my wedding. Our family is here, our friends are here, and this is actually one of the happiest days of my life.

CHAPTER SIXTEEN

THE LAST DINNER

MAGGIE CONROY

*W*e're having a ball. Everyone is seated at a banquet-size table. The windows with a view of the backyard have been covered, so I can't see what tomorrow is going to look like. Right now, Vince and I are with our closest friends and family members eating, laughing, talking, and drinking with Jack and Daisy, Charlie and Angel, Robert and Carter, Allie and her fiancé, Anne, Monroe, Cleo and her husband, Perry, who finally showed up, Hannah, and Lena Chance, who remained a friend of mine from the early days at A&Rt Media—she came with her husband, David.

"I remember the first day I saw you," Lena Chance says.

I smile squeamishly. "Uh-oh, what did you think?"

"Well, at first, I thought Rob must've hired you to get in your pants and Vince was taking the hit for him."

"That was typical," Robert says.

Vince grunts a chuckle in agreement.

"But then you proved you were a force to be reckoned with. I knew very quickly that I loved every part of you." She shrugs as she grins.

"I love you too, Lena," I declare.

"But, goodness, look how far we've all come," Daisy says.

"You know, love, it all started with you and me in Martha's Vineyard," Jack says.

Daisy smiles as she nods. "Right. At our 'shotgun wedding.'" Daisy laughs. "Belmont was so steamed when Maggie couldn't make it to our reception that he asked Vince if he had a job for you."

Vince puts his arm around my chair. "I said absolutely. I was already coming off feeling disappointed that you didn't recognize me in the elevator, Mags."

I shake my head. "You say that all the time."

"Yeah, well, I was very disappointed."

"Okay, then next, Charlie met Angel because of a referral from Jack," I say.

Monroe raises a finger. "By the way, I'm no longer bitter about that."

Charlie pretends to swipe the sweat from his forehead. "Whew, that's good to know, because I've been watching my back ever since."

Everyone at the table who knows how crazy Monroe can be laughs.

"Oh, and don't forget this one," Daisy says. "Robert leaves A&Rt Media and starts his own successful architect firm…"

"Congratulations again on that," Jack says.

Robert nods humbly. "Thank you and Thank you. You're the one who fed me the line."

Jack throws up his hands. "Hey, I knew you had it in you."

"It was pretty easy because the purchase came with some talented architects, although my best is no longer with me." Robert winks at Carter, and she rolls her eyes slightly.

Wow. Something *is* going on between them. I think they'll be great for each other.

"I don't know… according to the pattern of love luck, you might be next, Robert," Daisy says.

"I hope so," Hannah says.

Monroe grunts. "Let it go. Really, let it go." She shakes her head. "Anyway, what about me, though?"

"Your day is coming, Roe," I say. "None of us are here by accident. I look around the table, and this is exactly how it should be." I can't stop smiling, especially when Vince kisses me on the cheek.

CHAPTER SEVENTEEN

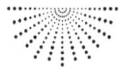

THE BIG DAY

MAGGIE ADAMS

*T*he ceremony starts in less than an hour. Last night, dinner continued into the wee hours of the morning. We had such a fantastic time. Thank goodness we had a mind to set the time of the wedding to five o'clock. Vince and I still haven't seen the venue. However, I know with all the talent involved in actually setting it up, it's going to look heavenly. The weather couldn't be lovelier. The sun has bestowed us with a perfect seventy-eight-degree day. I'm alone in my "bride's chamber" while the wedding party works on putting the final touches on everything. I absolutely love how all this came together. Our friends and family are the ones who planned our big day. And it's a big day indeed. I'm nervous, infinitely happy, and a little scared.

There's a soft rattle on the door.

"Come in," I say, trying to hide the shaking in my voice.

Anne's face peeps through the crack of the door first. "Hi, sweetie."

This is the first time she's called me that. "Hi, Anne."

She walks into the room and carefully shuts the door behind her. "I know you have a mother. She's out there making that very clear." She shakes her head a little. "But you can still call me Mom if you like."

I smile. "Thanks." One mother is enough to handle at the moment. Perhaps over time, I will call her mom.

"However, I would like for you to have this." Anne hands me a velvet necklace box.

I open it, and my jaw drops. Inside is a necklace with an encrusted diamond heart pendant. "This is for me?"

"Yes, it's just a little something old."

I'm just about to ask her to help me put it on when there's another knock on the door.

"Come in," I sing.

It's my mom. "Hi, darling."

"Hi, Mom." We hug.

"I can't believe what they've done out there. It doesn't even look like we're on earth. They've created a mystical, magical land."

"Oh, wow," I say, smiling more broadly. "I haven't even seen it yet."

My mom is frowning at the jewelry box in my hand. "What's that?"

"Oh, Anne gave me this. It's something old."

My mom doesn't even turn to acknowledge. I've never seen her behave so territorially before. I open the box.

My mom grunts as if she's not impressed. "I actually brought you this." She reaches into her purse. "My mom gave this to me on my wedding day, and now it's yours." She takes out another necklace box.

I glance at Anne before opening it. This is awkward, but I'm entitled to one moment like this on my wedding day. I grab my heart at the sight of the sparkly diamond necklace.

I look up at my mom with a befuddled expression. "Mom?"

"I want you to wear it today and then pass it on to your daughter or daughter-in-law when she gets married."

"Well," Anne says as if the sight of the diamond necklace took her breath away. "You must wear that gorgeous piece of jewelry."

Finally, Mom looks at her with a smile. "Thank you...."

"By the way, I'm Anne," Anne says.

"Anne, I'm..."

"Leah, I know."

"Yes," my mom says, glaring at her.

The women are back to squaring off.

Finally, they both leave, and Hannah helps me put on my dress and style my hair. This is also the first time I'm seeing the flesh-pink bridesmaid dresses. They're simple and beautiful, and Hannah had all the bridesmaids fitted with them this morning. She paid for them all, as well.

"I didn't know you people were so flush with cash," I say.

"You're not the only successful bitch in the group," Cleo says.

I share my last laugh with my beautiful group of friends before the wedding starts.

WE ALL TAKE OUR PLACES. MY HEART IS BEATING A mile a minute, and I think I might hyperventilate. I'm waiting behind the door to the backyard. My dad is standing beside me, ready to walk me down the aisle.

"Are you ready, princess?" he asks with watery eyes.

I smile. "I am."

"Can I get the first hug from the bride?" he says.

"Absolutely," I say, trying not to cry and mess up my makeup, which Hannah has flawlessly applied.

We hug. Someone knocks on the door. It's time.

The door opens, and the wedding march is being played by a section of harpists. After one step out onto the concrete, my eyes behold an unbelievable sight. The entire backyard is like an enchanted meadow. Deer are grazing on the grass, swans are swimming in the lake, and sheep are bathing in the sun. A bike with giant wheels and an open-top carriage awaits me. Jack and I climb in, and a man with a tight black suit, a pink rose pinned to his breast, and a mustache that curls at both ends pedals us down a sparkling gold street that was put in for this event. The closer we get, the more ethereal it looks. The bike drops us off near the lake, at the point where I'm to walk down the aisle. All of my brides-maids are there, including Monroe, who dubbed herself my maid of honor, which she truly is. I have one job. Walk down the aisle and then take my vows.

Vince is waiting for me at the front. I feel as though I'm having an out-of-body experience. So many people are here. There's Mavis and her husband. Did I invite Delta? Humph. He's here. There's Daisy and Jack, sitting in the front row, beaming. A couple dozen of our colleagues from A&Rt Media are here. Maddie and Lexie did end up attending. This morning before breakfast, I went to each of their casitas and practically begged them to come. I basically convinced them that if they missed this ceremony, they would regret it forever. Vince and I are never doing this again, with anyone else. They're smiling now, and that's a good sign. Vince has a boatload of friends and family. There are definitely more than a hundred people present.

Each face makes me more nervous than I was a second ago.

The last bridesmaid and groomsman walk down the aisle.

Robert whispers something to Vince, and he beams while staring at me. I think he's satisfied. I don't know. I have no idea how I'm existing in this moment.

"Let's go," I hear my Dad say.

All I can do is follow his lead. Finally, I connect with Vince's face. I'm choked up, and my tears are flowing. If only I could run to him and let him hold me tightly. One touch, and I know my nerves will calm.

The closer I get, the happier I feel, and I didn't think I could be happier. Monroe shows me a thumbs-up, and so do Hannah and Cleo. My smile spreads wider. Angel, who's also one of my brides-maids, blows me a kiss, and I catch it. Finally, I make it to Vince, and we hug.

Charlie puts up a finger. "I just have to…" He breaks from the line of groomsmen to give me a big fat hug.

"Congratulations, Magnolia." He kisses me on the cheek.

I can't stop crying. "Thank you, Chuck," I whisper past my tight throat.

Vince wraps his arms around me again. "It's going to be okay, baby," he whispers in my ear.

"It's just that I'm so happy to be doing this with you," I whisper.

He hugs me so tightly that I might break. "Thank you for loving me."

"Thank *you*."

The minister clears his throat. For some reason, everyone chuckles. He begins by saying how sacred marriage is. I remember how I rolled my eyes at Reverend Weasel during Jack and Daisy's ceremony. I'm not sure if I'm buying all that he's saying but I like it. In my mind and heart, Vince and I were married from the moment we made a true commitment in our hearts to work out our differences so that we can live happily together forever. The road was often bumpy, and we certainly needed that trip to Hawaii to learn that we are truly best friends. We made the love bond that is truly recognized by God a long time ago—the one that's made in the heart.

"Do you have words to say to each other?" the minister finally says.

My eyes grow wide. I have nothing prepared.

"I have something to say." Vince looks deep into

my eyes. As usual, his sexy green eyes leave me breathless. "Maggie, I knew from the first time I saw you that we would be standing like this together. You were made for me. I was made for you. I can't wait to finish spending the rest of our lives together."

I'm smiling so big, my face aches.

"And, Maggie, do you have words for Vince?"

At first, I can't think of anything to say. "Yes." I squeeze Vince's hands. "You're my best friend, forever lover, and the man I could've never dreamed of because I never knew love could be like this. We were two people who find each other unexpectedly, and now look at us. I love you, Vince. Nothing will ever change that."

We're staring into the each other's eyes, and the minister hasn't said anything yet.

"That's all," I say.

Everyone laughs.

The minister clears his throat. "Um, thank you."

Vince and I don't break eye contact. We're waiting for those famous words. Finally, they come.

"You may kiss the bride."

We embrace like there's no tomorrow and kiss

for the first time as a married couple. It's official—I am now Mrs. Vincent Adams.

EVERYONE MOVES INTO THE PAGODA TENT FOR THE reception. I am blown away by the decadence. The inside looks like a grand ballroom, with crystal chandeliers hanging from the high parts, silk table-cloths, and high-back chairs. There's a dance floor, and the biggest surprise of all is that Jacques Blanchard and his band are playing tonight. By luck, the only child present is in Daisy's stomach, so we eat. Then we cut the cake, dance, and drink rum and Mes Fleurs champagne. We are very merry as we party until the sun comes up.

I'VE LONG SINCE TAKEN OFF MY SHOES AND LET MY hair down. The band has agreed to give us two final songs. Charlie has been playing with them just about all night, while Angel has been keeping the dancing going. A slow melody hums in the air, and I'm dancing with Jack.

I take my head off his shoulder. "By the way, does Daisy know about your alter ego?"

He snickers. "Daisy knows everything about me."

"I assume that's a yes."

"I assume so."

I laugh and shake my head. "My cousin, the man who's always full of surprises."

Jack tosses his head back to laugh just as Vince taps him on the shoulder to step in.

"Where's my wife?" Jack says as he hands me to my husband.

"Here's my wife," Vince says, and we kiss.

"So this is it," I say.

He grins. "Yep, this is it."

"Hi, Mr. Magnolia Conroy." I kiss his lips.

"Hi, Mrs. Vincent Adams." He kisses my lips.

I rest my head on his chest, and we continue dancing until the last notes dissolve into silence.

ABOUT THE AUTHOR

Z.L. Arkadie's personality shines through in her books, which put a modern spin on romance. The Southern California based author's LOVE in the USA series follows an interconnected web of young professionals across the country as they establish their careers and navigate the pitfalls of love. Even when Arkadie puts a paranormal twist on her stories—as in the Parched series—she focuses on conversations and emotions that feel familiar.

For more information:
zlarkadiebooks.com
contact@zlarkadiebooks.com